John Arthur Fraser

Santiago

For the Red, White and Blue

John Arthur Fraser

Santiago
For the Red, White and Blue

ISBN/EAN: 9783337343415

Printed in Europe, USA, Canada, Australia, Japan

Cover: Foto ©Andreas Hilbeck / pixelio.de

More available books at **www.hansebooks.com**

SANTIAGO;

OR,

FOR THE RED, WHITE AND BLUE

A WAR DRAMA IN FOUR ACTS

BY

JOHN A. FRASER

AUTHOR OF "A NOBLE OUTCAST," "THE MERRY COBBLER,"
"OUR STARRY BANNER," ETC.

CHICAGO
THE DRAMATIC PUBLISHING COMPANY

CHARACTERS.

CAPT. OSCAR HUTTON, U. S. A.   In love with Cora......*Leading juvenile.*

LIEUT. FISK, U. S. A.   In love with his duty...................*Juvenile bit.*

MILTON MERRY, U. S. N.   In love with Bess..................*Light comedy.*

LIEUT. CRISTOBAL, S. A.   In love with soldiering..................*Straight.*

DR. HARRISON, Red Cross H. S.   In love with surgery...*Straight old man.*

ELMER WALTON, banker.   In love with Spanish bonds.

Character old man.

PHILLIP BASSETT, his stepson.   In love with Ysobel...............*Juvenile.*

FERNANDO DIAZ, Walton's cashier, afterwards S. A.   In love with Cora...*Heavy.*

BEVERLY BROWN, Walton's butler, afterwards Red Cross H. S.   In love with chickens...*Negro comedy.*

CORNELIUS DWYER, Walton's coachman, afterwards U. S. A.   In love with " Naygurs "...*Irish Comedy.*

ANTONIO CARLOS, a Cuban planter.   In love with Spain.

Character old man.

CORA BASSETT, Walton's stepdaughter.   In love with Oscar...*Juvenile.*

BESS WALTON, Walton's daughter.   In love with Milton........*Ingenue.*

YSOBEL CARLOS, Antonio's daughter.   In love with Phillip.....*Juvenile.*

American Soldiers, American Sailors, Spanish Soldiers, Guerillas.

———

Actual time of playing, two hours.

———

SYNOPSIS.

ACT I.—The ball at Walton's, Washington, D. C.   Handsome interior.

ACT II.—The Red Cross Hospital.   First day's battle of Santiago. Exterior.

ACT III.—Scene 1.—Interior.   Guerilla headquarters in the Sierra Cobra, near Santiago.   Scene 2.—Exterior.   The underbrush of the Sierra Cobra.   Scene 3.—Fight in the mountain pass, second day's battle of Santiago.   Exterior.

ACT IV.—Hotel Tacon, Santiago, on the night of the surrender. Interior.

NOTE.—Walton, Dr. Harrison and Carlos may double, easily, and the piece be played with nine males, three females.

AUTHOR'S NOTES ON PRODUCTION.

This is one of the easiest military plays that amateurs can produce, for a number of reasons. No special scenery is required ; every regular theatre in its ordinary equipment has every set called for by the manuscript, and, as the scene plots will show, novel and pretty effects will be secured. All the parts are comparatively short and not one of them is difficult to play. The three female parts are of equal strength, and there is not a particle of choice between them. The two character comedy parts are also equal, and they are very much in evidence all through the play. The military and spectacular features are very prominent, more so than in any other play within the reach of amateurs.

Thorough and painstaking rehearsal is necessary, because the situations are intense and striking, and there must be no hesitation, either for lines or business, when they are arrived at. The battle scenes, particularly, must be gone over again and again, with all the details, to make them so smooth as to seem like real war from the front of the house. Do not leave anything to chance. Rehearse until you know you are all right, both in your speeches and in your actions. The ends of the acts all require hard work, with everybody on the stage who is to take part in the performance.

Cora should be a blonde, Bess brown-haired, and Ysobel a decided brunette. Evening dress in the first act may be left to the individual taste of the actresses. The nurse dresses for the second and third acts should be white, perfectly plain, and with the red cross on the left arm, near the shoulder. Nurses' caps and white aprons are necessary. For the last act, to carry out the patriotic idea, Ysobel should dress in red, Bess in white, and Cora in blue—all evening dress. .

Hutton should look about 30 to 35. He wears infantry uniform all through. His is a strong part and requires an actor of some experience. In Act IV. his head is bandaged. .

Lieut. Fisk should look boyish, and he also wears infantry uniform.

ṢCENE PLOT.

ACT I.

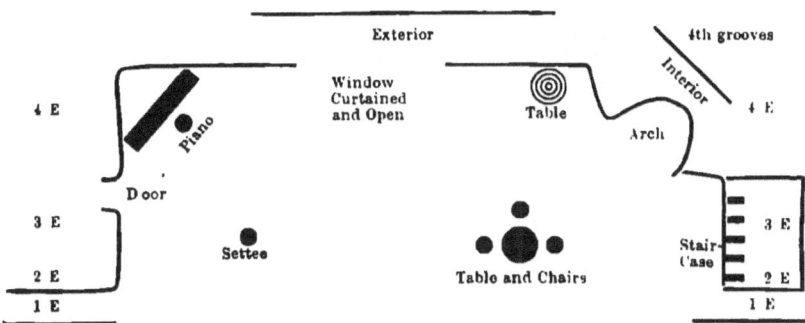

ACT II.

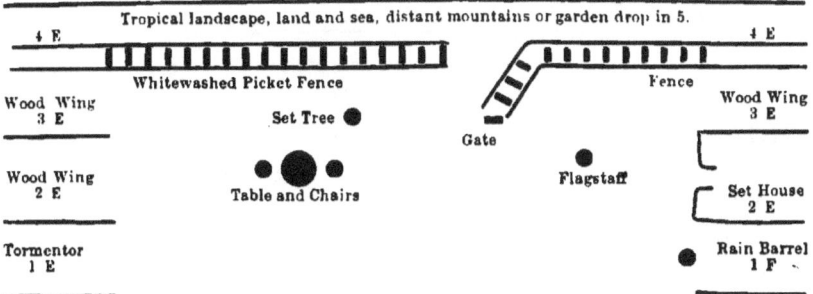

ACT III. SCENE I.

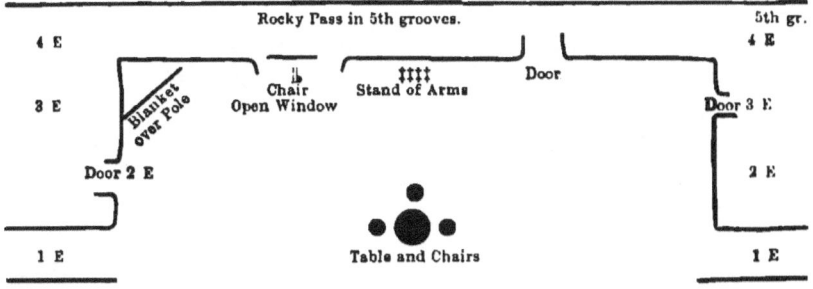

SCENE PLOT.—(Continued.)

ACT III. SCENE 3.

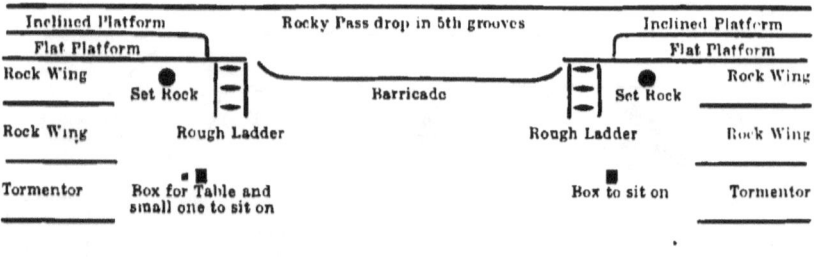

ACT IV.

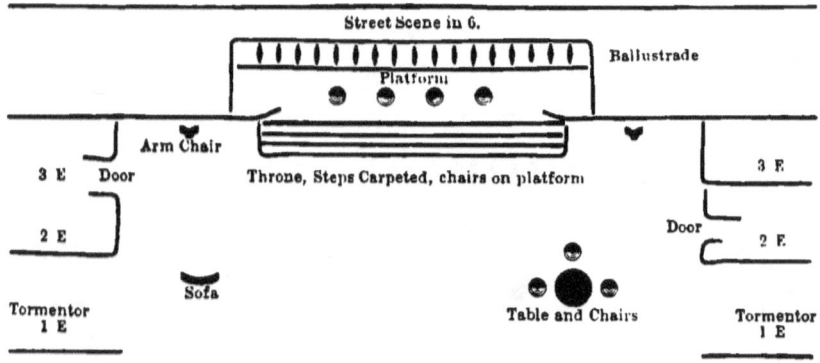

SANTIAGO;

OR,

FOR THE RED, WHITE AND BLUE.

ACT I.

[SCENE.—*Reception room in* **Elmer Walton's** *mansion, Washington. Lighted lamp on table,* L. C. *Piano open. Elegant rugs and furniture, bric-à-brac, etc. At rise of curtain* **Beverly,** *an old negro in evening dress and white gloves, is discovered turning up light of lamp.* **Corny,** *an Irish servant, also in evening dress, enters* L. I E.]

Bev. Well, fo' de Lawd's sake ! [*Laughs, pointing at* **Corny,** *whose suit is much too small, short in arms and legs.*]

Corny. Well, what the devil is the matter wid you ? [*Crossing to* C.]

Bev. Oh, look at dat suit—jes' nachelly look at it ! [*Laughs.*]

Corny. Oh, look at that naygur—look at that black naygur. [*Mocking* **Beverly's** *laugh and pointing at him.*]

Bev. Shet yo' head, Irish—shet yo' head. I's no niggah. I's a Cubian, dat's what I is.

Corny. Yer a *what ?*

Bev. I's a Cubian—dat's what I remarked, you cheap white Irish trash.

Corny. You a Cuban ! Listen to the Jim Crow dhramin' !

Bev. I wants yo' to understan' dat I was borned in Cuba ; yes, sah, and dat makes me a Cubian ; yes, sah, an' dat's what I remarked.

Corny. Oh, dear ! oh, dear ! Thin I suppose if you'd been born in Hong Kong 'twould have made you a haythen Chinee ! [*Sits on settee,* R. C.]

7

Bev. Shet yo' head. Who tole yo' to come in heah, any-way ? [*At table*, L. C.]

Corny. Your boss and mine—Misther Walton. I'm here to wait on the guests. [*Swelling.*]

Bev. [*In deep disgust.*] You wait on de guests ! *You !* Yo' better go out in de barn, whar yo' belong, an' wait on de hosses. Go out an' chew feed fo' sick mules—dat's all yo' fit fo', Irish.

Corny. I'll have your life for that ! [*Chases* **Bev.***, who dodges around table and around settee. He runs up stairway,* L. 2 E., *followed by* **Corny.** *Sounds of a scuffle. Angry voices are heard off and* **Corny** *falls downstairs, rolling over on stage.*]

Bev. [*After a pause, sticking head out of stairway.*] Say, Irish—is—is yo' dead ?

Corny. [*Sitting up.*] No ; I'm only spacheless.

Walton. [*Entering door*, R. 3 E.] What is the meaning of this noise ?

Corny. Sure, I jusht fell downstairs, assisted by that black naygur that calls himself a Cuban. He butted me like a goat. Oh, if I'd only landed on his shins !

Walton. [*Crossing to* C.] This constant quarrelling has got to cease or I'll discharge one of you. Now go and attend to the front door. That's *your* place. [*Ex.* **Corn.***,* L. U. E., *through arch.*] As for you, Beverly, you mind your own busi-ness and let Corny alone.

Bev. Well, let him keep still callin' niggah. I's no common niggah—I's a Cubian, dat's what *I* is. [*Ex.* L. I E. *Returns.*] An' dat's what I remarked. [*Ex.* L. I E.]

Walton. I wish that Cuban had emigrated before he brought on this war—with the Irish.

Corny. [*Without.*] Yis, sor—step inside, sor.

Walton. Ah, my guests are beginning to arrive. [*Looking off through arch.*] Diaz ! I'm glad he's come. [**Fernando Diaz** *enters through arch.*] You're early, Fernando. Any news ? [*Shaking hands. Bringing him down* C.]

Diaz. Yes. I came early on purpose to tell you that I have a cipher cable from Madrid. Spain has resources, hitherto unsuspected, both in Paris and Berlin, and the war will be pushed with vigor. Spanish 4's, which grew firmer to-day, will rise to-morrow, and I advise an early purchase.

Walton. But I'm carrying half a million of them now, with a big loss in the transaction to date. [*Sits* R. *of table*, L. C.]

Diaz. Buy another million and recover your loss on this rise. [*Sits on settee*, R. C.]

Walton. I'll think about it, and let you know before the evening is over. Has anything been heard of that young rascal ?

Diaz. Nothing. The detectives are quite discouraged. Mr. Walton, be guided by my advice for once—don't push this prosecution. Remember, he is your stepson.

Walton. [*Rising.*] I remember nothing, sir, except that he is a thief—that he has robbed me of over $50,000, and I shall punish him as I would any other forger and embezzler. You are too tender-hearted, Fernando, with a man who forged your name and did all he could to cast the suspicion and fix the crime on you.

Diaz. That is one reason why I ask mercy for him. Phillip and I were never friends. He disliked me, and it would look vindictive if I should seek to hound him down.

Walton. That is one reason. The other, and the principal one, is his sister, Cora. Eh, Fernando ? [*Sits down again.*]

Diaz. I certainly feel a great deal of sympathy for Miss Bassett—to say nothing of a warmer sentiment. Once more, Mr. Walton, in the name of your late wife, the boy's dead mother, let me beg of you to search for him no further. [*Rises during speech and crosses to* **Walton.**]

Walton. I am determined that if he can be caught he shall be punished. My only fear is that he may have left the country.

Diaz. But think of the disgrace to the family if he is tried and sent to the penitentiary.

Walton. Think of the disgrace to me, as a banker and business man, if he is *not*.

Diaz. You have done your duty. You have already expended fifteen hundred dollars.

Walton. I'll get him if it costs fifteen thousand. He squandered his share of his mother's fortune in reckless living and speculation. Then he began to steal. I'm glad my poor wife was wise enough to leave nearly all her money to Cora. By the way, how do matters stand between you two ?

Diaz. I make but little progress—yet I still hope.

Walton. That's right. A battle's never lost until it's won, and I am doing all I can for you.

Diaz. I know it. Thank you.

Walton. Who is the dangerous rival ?

Diaz. Captain Hutton.

Walton. [*Rises.*] Captain Hutton ! A man with the reputation of being the greatest lady-killer in the army! Surely you must be mistaken. Cora couldn't be such a fool.

Diaz. He is invited here, in spite of his reputation.

Walton. Yes, I know. One has to invite all sorts of people in Washington society. [*Hutton appears through archway in fatigue uniform. Aside.*] The deuce! Here he is. [*Aloud.*] Good-evening, Captain. We were just talking about you. [*Bus. of hand-shaking.* **Hutton** c., **Diaz** r., *and* **Walton** l. *of him.*]

Hutton. Nothing to my detriment, I hope?

Diaz. Oh, no! We were only wondering how soon you would be ordered to Cuba.

Hutton. The order has been given. We leave for Tampa immediately, and I have called to say good-bye instead of remaining to enjoy Mr. Walton's hospitality.

Walton. The ladies will be downstairs in a few minutes. So you are really off at last?

Hutton. Yes, at last.

Diaz. And you look for an easy victory, I suppose? [*Sneering. Sitting on settee.*]

Hutton. That is a subject on which I do not care to express an opinion to Señor Fernando Diaz.

Diaz. Oh, don't be delicate. I have lived in this country for fifteen years, off and on.

Hutton. Yes, but you are not yet a citizen—you remain a Spanish subject.

Diaz. Still, I'm not narrow-minded. If I think the United States has made a mistake in forcing this war, why, I think in good company. Any banker will tell you——

Walton. That it's an interference in matters that don't concern us, a waste of money and a terrible disturbance to business. [*Sits* r. *of table*, l. c.]

Hutton. Business be hanged! Two hundred and fifty-eight American sailors were foully murdered in Havana Bay, and the American people are going to avenge that crime if they have to *suspend* business till after they've done it!

Walton. That's all sentiment.

Hutton. Of course it's sentiment. It was sentiment that declared for independence in 1776. It was sentiment which declared that a British crew should not search an American ship in 1812. It was sentiment which declared that the shackles should fall from the limbs of three millions of slaves in this land of the free. And it is sentiment which now cries out, "Remember the Maine!"

Diaz. [*Rises.*] It is not sentiment, however, which will cause Europe to interfere in Spain's behalf and crush America's new-born ambition to rob my country of her island colonies. Self-interest—self-defence—will prompt the powers to call a halt.

Hutton. If the continental powers dare to interfere with anything this country wins in honorable warfare, the powers will have cause to regret it.

Diaz. What great event will happen then, Captain ? [*Sneering.*]

Hutton. The triumphant navies of the United States and England will sweep the seas, and dictate the peace and commerce of the world. [**Diaz** *laughs and sits down.*]

Walton. But if England should maintain a discreet neutrality ?

Hutton. By the time this war is over we'll be able to whip all Europe, single-handed, on the seas. As for invading America, there are a thousand ways for a foreign army to get in, but not one by which to get it out again.

Walton. If enthusiasm would annihilate armies and navies, Captain, the government need only attend carefully to your health, and keep you constantly in commission, to be quite invincible. [*Ladies heard laughing off* L. 2 E.]

Hutton. There are the young ladies now. [**Cora, Yso.** *and* **Bess** *enter by staircase*, L. 2 E. *Cross to* C.]

Cora. Why, Captain Hutton—in fatigue uniform ? [*Giving her hand.*]

Hutton. We've the word to move at last, Miss Bassett, so I'm in marching order. We leave to-night.

Bess. Oh, that hateful old Miles ! Sending you off to-night when you're engaged to me for two waltzes.

Cora. Let me present you to my Cuban friend, Miss Ysobel Carlos. [**Yso.** *and* **Hut.** *bow.*] Oh—and Mr. Diaz is here—I almost overlooked you. Mr. Diaz, Miss Carlos. [*A glance of recognition passes between* **Diaz** *and* **Yso.** *She bows very coldly.*]

Yso. [C.] Señor Diaz and I have met before—in Cuba.

Diaz. I seem to remember you, Señora—but——

Yso. Let me refresh your recollection, Señor. It was you who visited my father's plantation near Santiago, and telling him that you represented a syndicate of wealthy American sympathizers with the cause of Cuba Libre, offered to loan him **money on his property, with which to aid our struggling**

patriots. The papers were signed and the money paid. You left the plantation, but in less than an hour my father was arrested and the money *stolen* by Spanish guerilla soldiers. Strange—wasn't it ?

Diaz. [R. C.] Poor Señor Carlos—what a misfortune.!

Yso. That was more than two years ago, and he ha sbeen a prisoner ever since. At the time we did not suspect your good faith, but afterwards other wealthy patriots, who were too old to fight but still wished to do their share for Cuba Libre, were drawn into the same trap by you. They were also imprisoned and the money stolen.

Diaz. I simply pursued my business as a financial agent. What followed was none of my affair.

Yso. Perhaps not, but for all that my people in Cuba call you a treacherous Spanish spy and the tool of Weyler the Butcher. [*Goes up with* **Cora** *and* **Hutton.**]

Bess. [*Aside.*] What awful names they call that dear, good, patient man ! [*Goes up, meeting* **Milton Merry** *as he enters through arch. She shakes hands with him and they join* **Cora, Yso.** *and* **Hutton. Merry** *is in full dress uniform of naval cadet. After pantomime conversation,* **Cora** *and* **Hutton** *ex. door* R. 3 E. ; **Bess, Yso.** *and* **Merry** *at window.*]

Walton. I wasn't aware that you and **Cora's** protégé were acquainted. [*Still seated.*]

Diaz. [*Crossing to* **Walton.**] Nor I. Carlos is by no means an uncommon name, and I never thought ol connecting this girl with the daughter of Antonio Carlos. What brings her to Washington ?

Walton. Oh, like all the rest of these Cubans, she has a " mission." She is raising funds and enlisting nurses to equip an insurgent hospital on her father's place.

Diaz. With the Spanish in control at Santiago *I* shall probably have something to say about that. It was my own money that was loaned to Carlos, and as the interest has never been paid I can forfeit the property whenever I choose.

Walton. Cora and Bess are deeply interested in the hospital idea. Cora has given money, and both the girls want to go as nurses. [*Rises.*]

Diaz. And you ?

Walton. Have promptly put my foot down on that. I have no sympathy with this stupid form of hysteria which people call patriotism. But come, Fernando, I want to talk to you about that boy, Phillip. [*Takes him* R.] I have an idea he has gone to the Klondike. [*Ex.* R. 1 E.]

Diaz. [*Aside.*] I heartily hope he has. [*Ex.* R. 1 E.] Bess, Yso. and Merry *have been up at window. They now come down.*]

Bess. If Cora marries that Diaz, I'll cut her off my visiting list.

Merry. Don't be alarmed, Miss Bess—she won't. No true American girl would marry a sneaking Spaniard. [*Sits on settee,* R. C.]

Yso. [C.] He is a rascal. Of that I am sure. A spy for Spain and a thief for himself. He shared the plunder with the soldiers after they robbed my father, and doubtless made that a practice during his trip through Cuba, two years ago.

Bess. ·Father should know of this. [*Fixing the lamp shade on table.*]

Yso. And I intend that he shall. Through Fernando Diaz my father has been a prisoner in El Morro de Santiago for two years, and I hate him.

Merry. Never mind, Miss Carlos—*we'll* get the old gentleman out of trouble, for we'll blow El Morro to pieces.

Bess. We? What have you got to do with it? [*Somewhat startled.*]

Merry. My uncle, the senator, has got things fixed at last, and I'll be gazetted third lieutenant of the Gloucester to-morrow.

Bess. Thank goodness, you're going to Cuba. Oh! I'm so glad!

Merry. Oh, you're glad I'm going. [*Rises.*] Very well, Miss Walton, I hope I'll get killed.

Bess. [*Crosses to him.*] Oh, no—don't get killed—just wounded. [Ysobel *drops down to table and sits.*]

Merry. No—I'd sooner be killed, much sooner.

Bess. But if you get killed I can't nurse you. All I can do then is to water your grave with my tears, and cry till my nose is all red and I look like a fright. There's nothing romantic about a girl with a red nose.

Merry. Unless she's a lovely red Indian heroine in a Fenimore Cooper novel.

Yso. Seriously, Mr. Merry, Bess returns with me to Cuba as a nurse in my Clara Barton hospital. Possibly Cora will go, too.

Bess. But don't say a word to papa about it. He doesn't

know we've made up our minds yet, and there's apt to be trouble when he is told we're going.

Merry. Oh, I see. You're going in for nursing, and invite me to get myself wounded so that you can practise on me. How nice !

Bess. Isn't it ? Oh, I think it will be just lovely !

Merry. Delightful—for you.

Cora. [*Appearing at door*, R. 3 E.] Ysobel, Captain Hutton wants to ask you a question.

Yso. About my hospital ? Certainly. [*Ex. door*, R. 3 E.]

Merry. [*After watching her off.*] Thank heaven !

Bess. What for ?

Merry. She's gone. Now, Bess——

Bess. Who gave you leave to call me Bess ?

Merry. Nobody. Took it. Had to do it. Going away and have so much to say to you that I've got to economize time by dropping the " Miss."

Bess. Oh, indeed ! When are you going ?

Merry. In about a week.

Bess. In about a week ! [*Laughs.*] Well, in about *two* weeks you may call me Bess. Until then, don't forget your manners. Tra la la la. [*Sings and waltzes.*]

Merry. Now don't tease—please don't—not to-night. We may never meet again.

Bess. No such luck—bad luck, I mean.

Merry. Now please listen—I've been in love with lots of girls before——

Bess. You must have begun real young——

Merry. I did—I hadn't been at Annapolis a month before I was head over ears.

Bess. How many sweethearts have you had ?

Merry. Eleven—but——

Bess. Eleven ! *Eleven !*

Merry. That's all, but——

Bess. All but ! You should have been a Mormon, Mr. Merry.

Merry. Yes—a Merry Mormon. But I was never really in love till I met you, Bess, honestly.

Bess. Oh, you want me to be number twelve ! [*Laughs.*] No—I'm afraid you're too fickle for me. I hate fickle people.

Merry. Oh, honestly, I'm as true as steel. *I* wasn't fickle— it was the girls.

Bess. I see. You've been run over by Love's chariot eleven times, and now offer me the mangled remains of your heart. [*Laughs and sits on settee.*] I'm afraid you've been a little too promiscuous in your attentions.

Merry. Yes ; but think of all the experience I've had. Why, I can drive a shying horse with one hand. Every time I try to turn up the gas it goes out by accident, and I never carry matches.

Bess. Oh, but that isn't all. Of course, economizing the gas bill is very praiseworthy——

Merry. Isn't it ? And yet I've known the fathers of some of my sweethearts to raise an awful rumpus when I was only looking out for their own interests.

Bess. Some people are so—so—bigoted. [**Corny** *re-enters unobserved through arch.*]

Merry. [*Drops on his knees.*] Oh, Bess, don't send me away to the war without something to lend me courage. [**Bev.** *re-enters unobserved,* L. I E.]

Corny. [*Aside.*] An illegant thing for the courage is a sup of whiskey.

Merry. Say you'll wait for me until the struggle's over, and that if I come back safe and sound, with no discredit to my name, you'll marry me.

Bev. [*Aside.*] Listen to dem chilluns talking about marryin'! Gee, Lordy !

Bess. Well, of course, it's awfully nice to be engaged if you are both living in the same town, and all that—but—— . [*Sees* **Corny.** *Screams. Jumps up.*]

Bev. [*Rushing at* **Corny.** Get out of heah—get out of heah. How dast yo' stand heah an' listen to private conve'sashun ? **Bess** *and* **Merry** *make a rapid exit through arch,* **Merry** *shaking his fist.*]

Corny. The divil a private there was in that. Sure anybody wid ears could hear him.

Bev. Yo' go right back to yo' job at de do', an' deceive de guests. Yo' is under my orders inside de house. Yes, sah.

Corny. Under your orders ?

Bev. Yes, sah, dat's what I said an' dat's what I remarked. Now go on.

Corny. Not one step on your orders—[*Defiantly.* **Cora** *opens door,* R. 3 E.]—but merely because it's me jooty. [*Ex. through arch.* **Cora** *enters.*]

Cora. Beverly, will you tell papa I'd like to see him alone for a minute ? He's in the library with Mr. Diaz. [*Ex.* **Bev.**, R. I E.] I may as well tell him first as last. I'm of age and my own mistress, anyway.

Diaz. [*Re-entering* R. I E.] How charming you look this evening, Miss Bassett.

Cora. I'm sorry I can't return the compliment, Mr. Diaz. You look very much worried.

Diaz. I am. Shall I tell you why ?

Cora. Oh, I'm not at all inquisitive. [*Arranges chair* R. *of table to sit down, but stops as he finishes next speech and faces him.*]

Diaz. But I am going to tell you, for all that. I am worried about you.

Cora. About me ? How do my affairs interest you ?

Diaz. How can you ask ? You already know that I am madly in love with you, and it is only natural that I should be jealous of your good name.

Cora. You are talking Greek. I don't understand you. [**Hutton** *enters door*, R. 3 E.]

Diaz. Then I'll be plain. Captain Hutton is a dangerous man. For a woman to meet him in secret, and the fact to become known, is sufficient to ruin her reputation forever.

Cora. Go on, sir.

Diaz. For the past two weeks you have been meeting him secretly at an obscure hotel where there was little chance of your being recognized.

Cora. Well ?

Diaz. That fact having become known to me it may to others. There is only one course open to you. You must have a husband to shield you against the scandal which will follow. I offer you the protection of my name.

Cora. [*Slaps his face.*] There is my answer. [**Hutton** *comes down* C. *between them.*]

Hutton. [*Passing her up stage.*] Leave him to me.

Diaz. You !

Hutton. Yes, I. I could not avoid witnessing what passed between you and Miss Bassett a moment ago. To the stinging rebuke which she administered I have only to add that you are a cowardly liar, and that you have slandered the best and purest girl alive.

Diaz. Do you deny the meetings ?

Hutton. At present I am not answerable to you.

Diaz. You don't dare to answer.

Hutton. [*Strikes him in the face with his gloves.*] Demand an answer to that.

Diaz. I do. That insult calls for your blood or mine, and without delay. [*Goes* R.]

Cora. [C.] Oscar, if you love me, kill that cur. [*Pointing at* **Diaz.**]

Hutton. I intend to. Now retire while I arrange matters. Don't fear for me, darling. [*Conducting her to door,* R. 3 E., **Diaz** *crosses* L. *above table.*]

Cora. I am not afraid. See me before—before you meet him. [*Ex. door,* R. 3 E.]

Hutton. Now, sir, my time is short. I suggest that you drive to the club, secure a friend and return here for me. The terms can be arranged between our seconds on the way to the ground.

Diaz. Anything to secure speedy satisfaction. [*Ex. through arch. As* **Hutton** *turns to go* R. *door,* **Phillip** *appears at window. He is in private's infantry uniform.*]

Phil. Hist! Captain! [*Puts his rifle through window.*]

Hutton. Good heavens, Phillip—you must be mad to come here.

Phil. [*Gets through window.*] No, not mad—on duty, Captain. [*Salutes.*]

Hutton. But if your stepfather finds you here you will be arrested.

Phil. Had to risk it, Captain. The major wanted this note delivered, and as he knew I was your dog he sent me with it. [*Hands note.*]

Hutton. [*Opens note and reads.*] "We take train an hour earlier. Compelled to recall your leave." [*Looks at watch.*] Can't help it. I must stay to fight that fellow at any cost. [*Aloud.*] Get back to your company at once and tell the major I'll catch the regiment at the depot.

Phil. Can't I say good-bye to Sis?

Hutton. [*Up* L.] No—it's too dangerous. Mr. Walton may be here at any minute. [*As* **Phil.** *goes to window* **Cora** *and* **Ysobel** *enter door* R. 3 E. *and see him.*]

Cora. Phillip!

Phil. Sis! [*They embrace, up* R. *Tenderly to* **Ysobel.**] Are you afraid of me, Ysobel?

Yso. You know I'm not, Phillip. [*Gives her hands.*]

Cora. [*Nervously.*] My dear, dear brother—you must go —father——

2

Phil. [*They all work down stage.*] Don't call him that, Sis. He has never been a father to me. I have only three friends in the world—Ysobel, you and Captain Hutton, and, please heaven, I'll repay all your kindness and care of me by wiping out the stain upon my name, in the service of my country. [*He is* C. *with* **Ysobel**, *between* **Cora** *and* **Hutton**.]

Hutton. I know you will, my boy—I'm sure of it. Private Redbank will be heard from if an opportunity offers.

Phil. Thank you, Captain. [*Shakes hands.*] From this time on it's Private Redbank and Captain Hutton, with no allusion to the past. I know my duty and, God helping me, I'll do it till I fall with my face to the foe.

Hutton. I'm sorry you didn't find time to prepare that statement of your shortage in the bank. The day might come when your sister could use it in your favor.

Phil. I've got it. [*Handing paper to* **Cora**, *as they turn to go up.*] There it is, Sis—I sat up all last night to finish it, and it's correct within a hundred dollars, one way or the other.

Walton. [*Heard off* R. I E.] Then you must leave, for I'll not discharge Corny Dwyer.

Hutton. Mr. Walton—quick—the window ! [**Bess** *heard laughing off through arch.*]

Cora. Too late. Behind the piano ! [**Phil.** *hides behind piano, screened by* **Cora** *and* **Ysobel**. **Walton** *and* **Bev.** *enter* R. I E. **Bess** *and* **Merry** *enter through arch. During succeeding speeches* **Cora** *picks up* **Phil.**'s *rifle and smuggles it to him behind piano, unobserved.*]

Bev. I's powerful sorry you's got to lose my services, sah, but I's a Cubian, I is, an' I don't stan' fo' bein' called niggah by dat Irishman. nohow.

Walton. I don't suppose we'll have to close up the house when you leave. Now go and attend to your duties.

Bev. Yes, sah. [*Crosses and exits* L. I E. *Returns at entrance.*] I don't stan' fo' it nohow, sah—dat's what I remarked. [*Ex.* L. I E.]

Walton. Where is Diaz ? [*Sitting* R. *of table.* **Cora** *comes down and bends over his chair.*]

Hutton. [*Coming down with* **Merry, Ysobel** *and* **Bess** *up at window.*] He has driven to the club, but will return in a few minutes. [**Hutton** *has been earnestly pantomiming conversation with* **Merry** *from the moment he entered with* **Bess.** *Aside to him.*] May I depend on you ? [*As they sit* R. C.]

Merry. Is an apology impossible ?

Hutton. Out of the question.

Merry. Then I'll do my best. Ten paces, turn and fire. I never saw a duel, but I've read " The Field of Honor."

Hutton. He'll probably bring an experienced second. [*All this is aside.*]

Walton. [*Aside.*] Cora, you know my wishes regarding Mr. Diaz.

Cora. It is no use urging me, father. I don't like Mr. Diaz —I hate him.

Walton. You think he has been instrumental in my pursuit of your brother. On the contrary, he has done all in his power to induce me to drop the prosecution.

Cora. Then I think you are hard and cruel to ruin poor Phillip for the sake of a few paltry hundreds, which I would have paid long ago if I had only known the amount. [*Diaz returns through arch.*]

Walton. Paltry hundreds? His defalcation reaches away up into the tens of thousands, and the money was secured mainly by drafts on New York, bearing the forged signature of Diaz, as cashier. Diaz.

Diaz. What is it, sir?

Walton. What is the total of Phillip Bassett's default?

Diaz. $49,971.

Phil. [*Coming from behind piano.*] That is a lie. [*Has rifle.*]

Everybody. Phillip !

Phil. [*Coming down* C.] Yes, Phillip! And I repeat, that statement is a lie! I was fool enough and weak enough to use about $2,000 of the funds in my charge to protect margins which were afterwards wiped out. But if there is any such shortage as $50,000 in Walton's Bank, I have been made a scapegoat for another man—and I charge Fernando Diaz with being the real thief. [*Points at him. Band, bugle band or drum corps heard off in the distance, coming closer.*]

Diaz. That is false. Your forgeries are too clumsy to help you.

Cora. Here is a true statement of the amounts Phillip took, and the purposes for which they were used.

Walton. Lies—all lies.—Hold him till I telephone for the police. [*Diaz starts for* **Phil.**]

Phil. Stand back! I was on sentry duty this evening, and this gun is loaded. [*Backs up to window. Band is seen to pass window, followed by companies.* **Phil.** *gets through* *window.*]   Here's my company.   Good-bye, Ysobel, God bless you ! [*Falls in with passing company.* **Ysobel** *crying,* **Cora** *and* **Bess** *go up to window and wave him good-bye with hand-kerchiefs.* **Merry** *touches* **Diaz** *on shoulder.*]

   Merry.   We are ready.   [**Cora** *turns and sees this.*]

   Diaz.   There are two carriages at the door.   [*Going* L. U. E.]

   Merry.   [*To* **Hutton.**]   Come, Hutton.

   Cora.   Oscar !   [*Into his arms.*]

   Hutton.   Darling !

   [*During this the soldiers have continued marching past the window and the music has grown fainter and fainter.*]

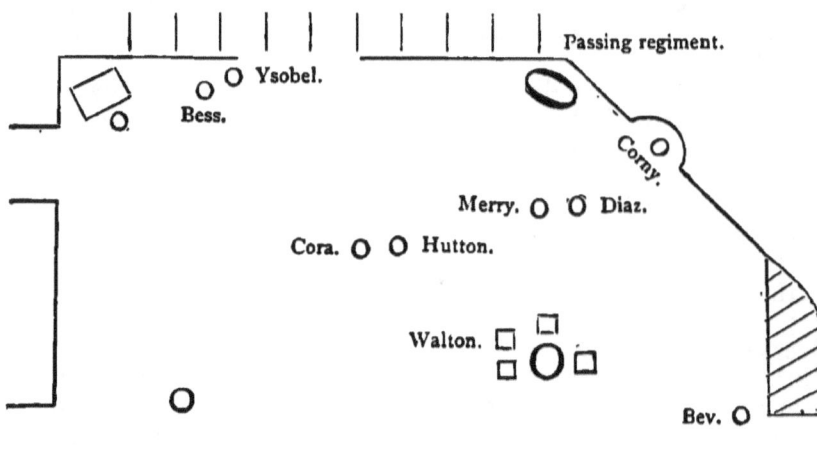

ACT II.

[SCENE.—*The Carlos plantation, near Santiago de Cuba. Foliage borders. Cuban flag on flagstaff with Red Cross flag above it. Lights full up at rise.* **Cora** *and* **Bess** *discovered up at gate looking off* R. *They wear white dresses, white nurses' caps and aprons, and have the red cross on the shoulder.*]

Cora. No sign of her yet. Oh, why did she insist upon undertaking such a perilous journey? [*They come down to table,* C.]

. **Bess.** Because there's no knowing what these treacherous Spanish guerillas may do. We must have a guard, either of Cubans or our own dear boys, to protect the poor fellows under our care. [*Sits* L. *of table.*]

Cora. But there was no real need for Ysobel to go alone. Enrico, Pedro, or any of them, could have got to Shafter's lines just as easily as she.

Bess. No, Cora. If the Spaniards caught any of the men they would probably shoot them. Disguised as a peasant, Ysobel is much more likely to make the journey in safety.

Cora. The wretches have murdered the sick and wounded in hospitals, and killed women and little children before this. Why should they hesitate now?

Bess. Because there are twenty thousand American soldiers on Cuban soil, and the Spanish don't *dare* to let loose their brutal instincts for fear of the grim vengeance that would follow.

Dr. Harrison. [*Enters from house.*] Well, nurse, we've lost another poor fellow.

Cora. Who?

Dr. H. José Prospero. He died five minutes ago. Starvation and exposure have done their deadly work at last. His wound would have been a mere trifle if he had only had a little strength left to throw off the fever.

Bess. He was such a good patient, too—so obedient and grateful for all we did. Poor José.

Cora. Are there any other critical cases, Doctor ? [*They are in a group*, L. C.]

Dr. H. No. I'm glad to say that, thanks to the intelligent and tender nursing you ladies are giving them, the others are in a fair way to recover.

Bess. That's good, Doctor. But nursing isn't half the fun I thought it would be. I've grown so accustomed to the sight of blood and suffering that I really believe I could chop a chicken's head off, now, without quivering a single quiver.

Bev. [*Entering with a bag over shoulder*, R. 1 E.] Chickens ? Is yo' talkin' about chickens ?

Cora. Why, Beverly, where have you been ?

Bev. I's been out foragin', Missy. Yes'm. Foragin'— dat's what I remarked. I's a Cubian, I is, an' I wasn't agwan to see dem po' brudder Cubians dyin' fo' de want o' chicken soup. No, ma'am. [R. C.]

Bess. But you didn't come to me. for any money, Beverly. [*Sitting* R. *of table*.]

Bev. Money ? Oh, sho ! g'long—what does a dahk complected Cubian want with money when it's chickens he's aftah ?

Cora. [L. C.] Beverly, you've been stealing. [*Very severely.*]

Bev. Stealin' ? Me steal ? No, ma'am—I's been foragin' —des nachelly foragin', dat's all. What's mo', I brung dem chickens. [*Opens bag and pulls out live chickens. Lets them escape.*] Hold on—hold on, Janiwerry ! [*Chasing chickens.*] You little fool—does you want dem Spaniels to git yo' ? [*Chases chickens off* L. 3 E.]

Dr. H. Where did you pick up that specimen, nurse ? [*Sits* L. *of table.*]

Cora. He was a servant in our house in Washington for years, and when Bess and I left home he came with us.

Dr. H. You'll excuse me for saying it, but I've often wondered what induced you and your sister to come to Cuba.

Cora. [*Leaning against middle of table.*] Bess is my stepsister, Doctor, and the story is not a pleasant one. My brother was in trouble, and in danger of arrest. Instead of running away from Washington he remained in hiding there, aided by a friend of mine in the army who eventually enlisted him, under an assumed name. The cashier of my stepfather's bank misconstrued my meetings with my brother and our good friend, and made a cruelly false charge against me. The consequence was a duel, in which the cashier was badly wounded by my army friend, and in the unpleasantness which followed Bess sided with me against her father. Ysobel interested us in the Red Cross work, and here we are.

Dr. H. That is romantic enough, surely.

Bess. Oh, Cora's always having something romantic happen to her. Nobody ever fought a duel for me. [*Merry, with a party of ten sailors, enters* L. U. E. *They march to gate and come down.*] And I'm just dying for a little romance.

Cora. Look! [*Pointing to sailors.*]

Bess. Our guard! Oh, lovely. I wonder if their officer is nice?

Merry. Halt! [*Sailors halt,* L. C. *Merry turns.*] What! Bess!

Bess. Oh—Milton! [*Runs to him,* L. C. *Gives him both her hands.*] I'm so glad it's you.

Merry. And I'm so glad it's *you*. And Miss Bassett, too! [*Crossing to* C. *and shaking hands.*] Well, who would ever have thought of finding you two here?

Bess. Oh, you didn't come to see me?

Merry. I cannot tell a lie. I didn't know you were in Cuba. We are on our way to General Shafter with important information, and the boys are tired and hungry. We saw by the flag that this was a Cuban hospital, so we thought we'd stop here to rest and get a bite to eat.

Bess. Dr. Harrison, this is Lieut. Merry—an old friend of ours.

Dr. H. [*Shaking hands.*] So I perceive. Glad to know you.

Bev. [*Re enters with a pair of chickens in each hand.*] Dey cain't git away now, 'cause dey legs is tied. Well, fo' de Lawd's sake! [*Looks at sailors. Sees* Merry.] An' if it ain't Mars Milton! Well, bress my black soul! [*Drops the chickens and shakes hands.* Bess *and* Cora *go* R.]

Merry. What are you doing here, Beverly?

Bev. I always tole yo' I was a Cubian, didn't I? Yo' done heard me remark dat befo'?

Merry. I believe I did. [*Down* C.]

Bev. Well, I's quartermaster in de Cubian army an' in charge of dis yer hospital. I kinder shaperoons de young ladies and attends to de cookin'—yes, sah. You des ought to see me in mah unicorn—I's fairly gorgeous. Yes, sah.

Cora. Do you think you could give these men something to eat, Beverly?

Bev. Could I ? What's de mattah with fresh bread, sweet taters, coffee an' fried chicken ? En, boys ?

Sailors. What's the matter with Beverly ? He's all right !

Bev. [*Picks up chickens.*] Den foller me. I's a Cubian, I is, an' a Yankee sailor is de bes' friend I got. [*Sailors cheer.*]

Merry. Break ranks. [*Sailors ex. with* **Bev.** *into house.*]

Cora. Doctor, don't you think we'd better see that the boys are comfortable ?

Dr. H. [*Glancing meaningly at* **Merry** *and* **Bess,** *then at* **Cora.**] Nurse, when it comes to making people *comfortable* you have no equal. [*They ex. into house.*]

Bess. Well ?

Merry. Well ?

Bess. Is that all you've got to say ?

Merry. Is that all *you've* got to say ?

Bess. Do you know what's the matter with you, Milton Merry ?

Merry. No. What is it ?

Bess. You *talk* too much. [*Sits on table. Looks around.*] We're all alone.

Merry. [*Looks around.*] That's a fact. Are you scared ?

Bess. No. But you seem to be.

Merry. Things are seldom what they seem. You can't scare me.

Bess. [*Archly.*] There's nobody looking. [*Holding up her face to be kissed.*]

Merry. [*Looks around.*] Not a soul. What are you looking up there for ?

Bess. Something I haven't got, stupid.

Me ry. Can I get it for you ?

Bess. You've got it, but you won't give it to me, you hateful thing. [*Looking up.*]

Merry. [*Aside.*] I wonder whether she'd get mad if I kissed her ? Well, I don't care if she does. [*Kisses her.*]

Bess. [*Looks at him. Looks up again.*] More ! [*He kisses her again. Same bus. repeated.*] More ! [*He kisses her again.*] And you told me you'd had eleven sweethearts, could drive a shying horse with one hand, and always turned out the gas by accident when you went to turn it up. You're a fraud, Milton Merry. A Merry deceiver.

Merry. I admit it. That was all a jolly. I made it up. But I've quit lying, Bess—you are the only girl I ever kissed.

Bess. [*Laughs.*] Now you've gone too far on the other tack. I can't believe that.

Merry. It's the solemn truth. I never had nerve enough to make love to a girl till I saw you. All I told you I picked up from the other fellows at Annapolis.

Bess. You were only bragging? [*Gets off table.*]

Merry. That's all. You are the only girl I ever really wanted to kiss. I love you.

Bess. Then kiss me again. [*He does so. She puts first one of his arms and then the other around her.*] There. Isn't that nice?

Merry. Heavenly! I'll stop here and starve to death, but I'll die happy.

Bess. Oh, you poor fellow! I can smell that chicken frying —come along.

Merry. [*Detaining her.*] Wait a minute.

Bess. What for?

Merry. This. [*Takes ring off his finger and puts it on hers.*] There. Now—are we engaged?

Bess. Well, if we're *not*, these proceedings have been highly improper, and I'd better get what Beverly calls a "shaperoon." [*They ex. into house laughing.* **Diaz** *enters* R. U. E., *with a lieutenant carrying a flag of truce ; eight soldiers carrying stretchers follow. Men in the four stretchers. All Spanish guerillas.*]

Diaz. [*After leading them down and across* R.] Halt! [*They halt.*] Our information seems to be correct. The place is unguarded. Our object is to get inside and, after disposing of these Cuban dogs, to take possession. No quarter, remember. Let none escape. Kill them all, but use the steel, as we have only a few rounds of ammunition left.

Lieut. Cristobal. What about the women? [C. *with* **Diaz.**]

Diaz. If they're pretty, deal gently with them. The head nurse is Cora Bassett, and she is my prize. You may take your pick of the others. [**Lieut. C.** *salutes.* **Dr. H.** *and* **Cora** *enter from house.*]

Cora. Diaz here! [*Turns to retreat.*]

Diaz. Wait, Miss Bassett. [*Crosses* L.] You wouldn't be so unkind as to turn your back on an old friend. [*Offers his hand. She puts hers behind her.*]

Cora. You were never a friend of mine, Captain Diaz.

Diaz. You are right—friendship faintly expresses what I have always felt for you. Who is in charge here?

Dr. H.   I am chief surgeon.   [*On the steps.*]

Diaz.   I have brought you some patients.

Dr. H.   We haven't sufficient accommodations for our own sick and wounded, sir.   The hospital is overcrowded now.

Diaz.   You refuse to receive my men ?

Dr. H.   I am compelled to.

Diaz.   Then I shall take possession in the name of Spain.

Cora.   You can't.   We are under the protection of the International Red Cross, and this building is sacred.

Diaz.   This building is *mine*.   You have occupied it without my consent.   Lieut. Cristobal, haul down those rags and run up the Spanish flag.   [**Lieut. C.** *salutes and goes to flagstaff as* **Diaz** *crosses* R.]

Cora.   [*Stopping* **Lieut. C.**]   Stop !   [*Pointing.*]   There flies the ensign of humanity.   There floats the banner of freedom. You shall not displace them for the red symbol of cruelty and the yellow emblem of tyranny.

Diaz.   [R.   *Laughs.*]   Who'll prevent it ?   Up, men !   [*Men on stretchers jump up and fall in line.*]

Cora.   Treachery !   Inside, Doctor.   [*She runs into house followed by* **Dr. H.**, *closing door.*]

Diaz.   [*Laughs.*]   That's where I want you, my dear. You're mine now and nothing can save you.   [*Goes to flagstaff to lower flags.*   **Merry** *and sailors enter* L. 1 E.]

Merry.   Give it to them, lads.   "Remember the Maine !" [*Sailors fire.   Spaniards yell and run off* R. 2 E. *with* **Diaz.** *Sailors cheer.*]   They're on the run, lads.   Keep them going. Charge !   [*Sailors cheer and follow* **Merry** *off* R. 2 E.   *Shouts and shots are heard,* R.   **Cora, Bess** *and* **Dr. H.** *re-enter from house.*   **Ysobel** *enters* R. U. E.]

Cora.   Ysobel !   [**Yso.** *staggers.*   **Cora** *and* **Dr. H.** *go up and catch her.*]   What has happened ?

Yso.   [*Supported by* **Dr. H.**]   The Spaniards !   They pursued me.   They are in force.   This firing will bring them down upon us.

Cora.   Did you reach Shafter's lines ?

Yso.   Yes.   He promised us immediate help.   The Americans are moving forward.

Cora.   Then we'll defend our wounded till aid arrives.   We have arms and ammunition, and I, for one, am not afraid to use them.   [*Comes down.*]

Yso.   Nor I.   [*Follows* **Cora** *down.*]

Bess.   Nor I ; and if they hurt Milton Merry let them look out.

Dr. H. You are three brave girls and you may depend on me.

Bev. [R. C.] An' me. I ain't no good on de shoot [*Draws a white-handled razor*] but when it comes to cuttin' an' carvin'—ziz! ziz! [*Slashing with razor.*] I's a Cubian by birth, but a Darktown coon by edication. [**Merry** *and sailors enter* R. U. E., *retreating and firing as they cross to gateway. Distant bugle calls and sound of cannon heard. They come down.*]

Merry. [*At back.*] Cease firing! Listen! [*Distant cannon.*] Hurrah! They've heard it, too. [*Cannon.*] See, see—they're falling back on their main body. It means a general engagement and they'll let us alone for a time, at least. [*Comes down.*]

Bess. What are you going to do? [*The sound of cannon and musketry comes closer.*]

Merry. Well, as it is impossible for us to get through to Shafter, with two or three thousand Spaniards in the way, the best thing we *can* do is to wait here till he comes up. [**Ysobel, Dr. H.** *and* **Cora,** C., *under tree.*]

Dr. H. We had just determined to defend this place till the last.

Merry. [*Cannon heard.*] By the sound of things a hospital will be a pretty important point in a very short time. We'll help you to hold it.

Ysobel. The advance on Santiago has begun, and we shall be within the American lines before midnight. [*Shots heard off close by.*]

Merry. Here they come. Don't expose yourselves, lads, and so draw their fire on us. Scatter among the trees and keep under cover.

Sailors. Ay, ay, sir. [*They ex.* R. *Shots heard.*]

Bess. [L. C. *Sees blood on* **Merry's** *hand.*] Oh, Milton, you are wounded! Come inside and let me bandage it.

Merry. I haven't time. It's only my left arm, anyway.

Bess. But I insist. Let me see it. [*Pulls off his jacket. His left sleeve is bloody.*] Oh, you poor fellow! Doctor, look here.

Dr. H. [*Examining arm.*] The bullet went clean through, but, fortunately, without striking a bone. [**Bess** *brings bowl of water from rain barrel and sponge and bandage from house. She assists doctor to bandage wound,* C. *under tree.* **Cora, Yso.** *and* **Bev.** *up looking off* R. *Shots heard continuously.*]

Yso. [*Up at fence looking off* R.] Look—look ! The Spaniards are retreating. They are coming this way. [*She comes
down with* Cora *and* Bev. *They go into house and return
immediately with guns. Cannon heard.*] They are shelling
the woods.

Bess. Milton, you must come inside. It's dangerous here.

Merry. Then this is where I belong.

Bess. But you are disabled.

Merry. [*Aside to her.*] If there weren't quite so many
people about I'd prove the contrary. [*Spanish soldiers enter
hurriedly* R., *in twos and threes, cross and ex.* L. *as if retreating. Cannon heard. Shell with lighted fuse is thrown from* •
R. *and falls* L. C. . *The girls scream and* Bev. *falls on his
knees, praying.* Ysobel *picks it up and drops it into rain
barrel with a splash. This occurs while the retreat is in
progress.*]·

Dr. H. Nurse, you're a heroine. If that shell had exploded
it would have torn the house to pieces and probably killed us
all.

Merry. Señora, that's the coolest thing I ever saw. You're
a daisy. Hello ! she's fainted. That's just like a woman—as
strong as iron one minute and as weak as water the next.
[*While* Dr. H. *and* Cora *are reviving* Yso. *he looks into barrel.*]

Bess. [*Terrified, pulling him away.*] Milton ! Come
away ! It might go off—oh, it might go off !

Merry. Don't be alarmed, my dear—you could no more
shoot the horns off the new moon with a popgun than set that
thing off now. It's too damp wet.

Bess. How dare you swear before me, sir ?

Merry. I didn't. I said damp—wet. [*Cheering heard off*
R., *distant at first and coming closer. Spaniards are now
running across from* R. *to* L. *A regiment of American soldiers enters on the double, in pursuit, cheering.* NOTE: *Both
Spaniards and Americans cross, recross behind the back
drop, and cross again. By this mean a company of soldiers
can be made to represent a brigade, and the movement be kept
up without interruption for an indefinite period. During
this scene American soldiers enter with wounded on stretchers,
R. 3 E. and* R. 2 E., *and are led into house by the girls,* Dr. H. *and*
Beverly. *After the soldiers are all off* Merry *blows his whistle.
Sailors re-enter* R. *Only the sailors,* Bess *and* Merry *on the
stage. The sailors line across stage up* L.]

Bess. What are you going to do ?

Merry. Push on to Shafter's headquarters, now that the Dons have made themselves scarce. I've got to obey orders, my dear.

Bess. But who's going to protect *me ?*

Merry. I'll see that you have a guard here and I'll get back as soon as I can. Fall in. [*Men fall in line.*] About face. [*They face up stage.* **Merry** kisses **Bess.**] Right face. Forward—march. [*Ex. with sailors through gate and off* R. U. E.]

Bess. [*Watching them off and waving handkerchief.*] That dear boy ! I wonder what makes him so much nicer here than he used to be at home ? I guess it must be the climate. [*Comes down.*] Well, if anybody had told me this morning that I'd be engaged to Milton Merry before night I'd have said, "You're crazy." Oh, well, I suppose man proposes, and woman disposes.

Bev. [*Entering from house.*] 'Scuse me, Missy Bess.

Bess. Well, what is it, Beverly ?

Bev. Does yo' think dey's liable to be any mo' Spaniels round heah dis evenin' ?

Bess. It's hardly likely after the whipping they got this afternoon. Why ?

Bev. 'Case dem po' wounded brudder Cubians didn't git a smitch of dem chickens after all. De sailor men done et up even de bones.

Bess. Well ?

Bev. Well, I knows whah dey's a chicken roost owned by one of dem rich old Spaniels, an' I was figurin' on ticklin' dey feets in de dark of de moon.

Bess. I see. You want to go and rob a henroost.

Bev. No, indeedy ! I's jined de chu'ch. Yes'm. *I* wouldn't rob no henroost. I des nachelly wants to go foragin' fo' de benefit of dem po' wounded men. What's mo', I's feelin' kinder chicken hungry myself. Yes'm. Kin—kin I go, Missy ?

Bess. I think you'd better stop here, Beverly. That hateful Diaz and his men are still in the neighborhood, and if he ever catches *you*——

Bev. De Lawd have mussy on my brack hide ! Reckon he'd skin me alive. Dat cullud lady won't see me to-night. No, ma'am.

Bess. Oh ! So there's a colored lady in the case, is there ? I thought it was chickens.

Bev. De lady done promised to show me whah dem chickens roost low, Missy. *[Men carrying wounded man on stretcher enter* R. I E., *and stop* C.] Gee Lawdy ! Heah's another dead man. [**Cora** and **Dr. H.** *re-enter from house.*] Dis is what dey calls glory.

Cora. Poor fellow. *[Looking at him.]* He has fainted.

Dr H. *[Examines wounded man.]* Shot through the shoulder and wounded in the head. *[Raises him.]*

Cora. *[Raising bloody bandage from his face.]* Merciful heaven ! My brother ! Phil—Phillip—speak to me.

Bess. Oh, Cora ! Poor Phillip. *[Puts arm around* **Cora.**]

Phil. Sis—kiss me—I'm afraid—I'm going. Hold my hand, Bess – I'm—I'm done for. *[Falls back fainting.* **Cora** *kisses him. Both girls crying.* **Ysobel** *enters from house. She goes to stretcher, sees* **Phillip.**]

Yso. Phillip—Phillip ! Dead ! My love ! *[Kisses him.]*

Dr. H. He is weak from loss of blood and has fainted, that's all. Carry him inside, boys. *[They do so.* **Yso.** *goes in with them.*]

Cora. Is there any hope, Doctor ? Tell me the truth. *[Crying.]*

Dr. H. He will recover. His wounds are serious but not mortal. You remain here and let Ysobel help me while I look for that bullet. You are too nervous and excited to be of much assistance. *[Ex. into house.]*

Cora. *[Drying her eyes.]* No ! I'm not a coward. He is my brother and I'll be cool and brave for his sake. *[Ex. into house. Men off* R. *in distance heard singing " A hot time in the old town to-night."]*

Bess. *[Runs up and looks off.]* More soldiers ! Oh, doesn't that tune sound good ! It's like a strain across the sea from home. I feel better already.

Bev. Dey's marchin' fo' Santiago, an' if dey reach it dey'll be a hot time, sho' 'nuff. *[Company marches on* R. U. E., *singing, headed by* **Hutton.**]

Hutton. Halt ! Yes. This is the place at last. *[At gate. To* **Bess.**] Can you tell me, Miss——

Bess. Why, Captain Hutton !

Hut. Miss Walton ! *[Comes down through gate and shakes hands.]* This is indeed a delightful surprise. How long have you been here ? *[They come down.]*

Bess. Only a week, but we've seen plenty of service, even in that short time.

Hut. My company has been detailed to guard this hospital, and I was told to report to the head nurse.

Bess. She'll be here in a moment. But didn't you receive Cora's letter, telling you that I was coming here with Miss Carlos?

Hut. Not a line. The post-office arrangements have been a good deal mixed.

Bess. That's strange. We sailed before you did, and were landed at night by a Cuban pilot, after running the blockade.

Hut. And how did you leave Cora? Well and happy?

Bess. Oh, she was all right the last time I saw her. [*Mischievously.*]

Hut. Well and happy, God bless her! What was she doing, Bess? I'm hungry to hear about her.

Bess. She was—you won't get mad, now—will you?

Hut. Why, of course not.

Bess. Well, just about the last I saw of her, she was kissing another man.

Hut. I don't believe it. You're not in earnest. She couldn't have forgotten so soon.

Bess. You don't believe me, eh? Beverly.

Bev. Yes, Missy. Sarvent, Cap'n. [*Saluting. He has been listening and grinning.*]

Bess. You remember the last time you and I saw Miss Cora?

Bev. Sho'ly, Missy.

Bess. Didn't she kiss that man?

Bev. She sho'ly did. Yes'm.

Bess. Now, sir, I hope you're satisfied. You gentlemen are a little too apt to imagine yourselves what Beverly calls the "Onliest." Well, I'll tell the head nurse you're here, if you like.

Hut. Thank you. [*Aside.*] She's forgotten me. [*Sits* L. *of table.*]

Bess. [*Aside.*] I think I've paid him back for the way he used to tease the life out of me. [*Ex. into house, followed by* **Bev.**]

Hut. What a fool I was to think her different from other ➡ women. [*Calls.*] Lieutenant Fisk, you may move the company under the trees, yonder [*Pointing* R.], and post your sentries at once. See to it yourself. [**Lieut.** *gives orders and marches the company through gate and off* R. 2 E., **Hut.**

watching them. **Cora** *enters from house, crosses to him. His back is toward her.*]

Cora. You sent for me, sir ? [*He turns.*] Oscar !

Hut. Darling ! [*Embrace.*] I understand it now. Phillip has been brought here.

Cora. Yes. We have just dressed his wounds.

Hut. And you kissed him ?

Cora. Of course I did. He's my own brother.

Hut. Wait till I get hold of Bess, the little schemer. I'll fix her, and that " *Cubian*," too. How is Phillip ? Is his wound severe ?

Cora. The bullet has been extracted from his shoulder, and he is resting easily. It was only a spent shot.

Hut. Yes. He got it in the skirmish line. He is behaving splendidly and is as brave as a lion.

Cora. I'm glad to hear that. But what do you think ? Diaz was here to-day just before the engagement began.

Hut. Diaz ? I thought I had killed him. Then he didn't die ?

Cora. No. He has quite recovered and is now a guerilla captain. He attempted to take possession of this place, but fortunately Mr. Merry was here, with a party of sailors, and drove the Spaniards off.

Hut. So the fellow has shown his true colors at last ! Undoubtedly, he was one of the corps of spies, acting under Dubosc, which kept Sagasta informed of every move made by our government. [**Lieut. Fisk** *marches on* R. 3 E. *with* **Corny** *and two other soldiers, mounting guard. Begin to darken the stage.*]

Lieut. Fisk. [*At gate.*] Halt ! Your instructions are to patrol post Number 2, from the big tree to the stone wall. Let nobody pass through the lines in or out without the correct password and countersign. Relief, forward—march. [*Marches off with the other two soldiers,* L. 3 E.]

Corny. Liftinnant—Liftinnant, darlin'. Whin do I ait ? He's gone, and here I am left to die wid the hunger. [*Patrols back and forth along fence.*]

Cora. Surely I know that brogue.

Hut. You ought to. It's Corny Dwyer, your old coachman. He followed your brother Phillip into the service and is devoted to him.

Cora. [*Goes up.*] Corny ! Don't you know me ?

Corny. Well, for the Lord's sake—'tis Miss Cora ! Gineral salute—presint arms ! [*Presents arms.*] Tell me, ma'am—

did you hear ere a word about young Masther Phillip? Sure he got hurted. [*Lights half down.*]

Cora. They brought him here and he is doing nicely.

Corny. Glory be! Now, I'm aisy ag'in, for I'll see him as soon as me time on sintry go is up.

Cora. Didn't I hear you complain of being hungry?

Corny. Faith I am—and thirsty, too.

Cora. Then I'll send you something to eat.

Corny. And *drink*, ma'am. Oh, if this was only Kentucky! [*Stage is darkened by this time.*]

Cora. Oscar, will you come in and see Phillip?

Hut. Certainly. And how is Miss Carlos? [*As they come down to house.*]

Cora. As enthusiastic as ever for Cuba Libre, and in love with the whole American army. She knows every foot of the country about here, and has already been of great service to our forces by obtaining information. [*They ex. into house.*]

Corny. Well, if there's anything I love 'tis walkin' up and down wid a gun in me hand and a stomach full of wind and wishes. [*Stops at gateway.*] Oh, but I was the foolish man to lave me horses and comforts to come here. [**Lieutenant** *enters* L. 3 E., *and crosses to ex. by gate.*] Halt! Who goes there?

Lieut. Officer of the day.

Corny. Officer of the day, what the divil are you doin' out here at night?

Lieut. Stand aside, sentry, and let me pass.

Corny. The divil a pass till you give the password. [**Lieut.** *whispers to him.*] That's all right. Pass, officer of the day. [*Saluting.*]

Lieut. I only wanted to see if you knew your business, Dwyer.

Corny. Faith, I ought to, Liftinnant. I served sivin years in the 88th Connaught Rangers, before I left the ould counthry.

Lieut. Well, see that you don't loiter on your post. Keep moving. [*Ex.* R. 2 E.]

Corny. Kape movin'! The divil a thing have I done since daylight, only kept movin'.

Bev. [*Enters from house with lunch on a tray.*] Now, wha's dat sojer man? Oh, I see him. [*Goes up.*] Heah, sojer man. I done brung you some lunch.

Corny. Hello, Beverly, ye black divil, how are ye?

Bev. Who's yo' callin' black debbil?

Corny. You, you naygur. Don't you know your ould frind, Corny Dwyer?

Bev. Well, fo' de Lawd's sake—is dis really you?

Corny. What's left of me. But come on down to the end of me post till I get me hooks into that grub, where the Liftinnant won't see me.

Bev. No, sah. I's quartermaster in de Cubian army and chief steward of dis yer hospital, an' I don't take no black debbil nor no niggah from nobody, no mo'. You's got to 'pologize or go hungry. [*Turns to go to house.*]

Corny. Well, I suppose a naygur's as good as another here, so I apologize. This ain't the United States.

Bev. No. Dis ain't de United States—not yet. But it soon will be, you bet. [**Corny** *grabs something off the tray and begins to eat.*] Heah, heah—come on, whah you can eat like folks. [*Ex.* L. 3 E., *followed by* **Corny.**]

Diaz. [*Enters sneaky,* R. U. E.] They are off their guard. Good! A few shots will draw them away from the house to see what the cause is, and while they're gone I'll secure my pretty Cora and carry her off to my headquarters in the mountains. Once clear of the highway they can never follow us in the darkness. Now to give the signal for the fusilade. [*Fires revolver twice and exits* R. U. E. *Shots are at once heard off* R. *in the distance. Bugle call, the assembly, is sounded off* R., *close by.* **Lieut.** *re-enters* R. 2 E. *as* **Hutton** *enters from house.*]

Hut. What is that alarm, Lieutenant?

Lieut. I don't know, sir. I was just going to see. [*More shots in distance.*] Listen!

Hut. It's a night attack on Hill's position. We must reinforce him, for if he is wiped out the hospital is at their mercy. Come on. [*Exit with* **Lieut.**, R. 2 E. **Cora, Ysobel** *and* **Bess** *enter from house.* **Diaz** *and his men are creeping along behind picket fence toward gateway.* **Corny** *and* **Bev.** *re-enter* L. 3 E. *Shots heard off* R.]

Yso. There it is again. The Spaniards have renewed the attack.

Cora. We are perfectly safe here. Captain Hutton will protect us. [**Diaz** *and his men suddenly spring through gateway.* **Bev.** *and* **Corny** *are knocked down.* **Diaz** *leads.*] What do you want here?

Diaz. You, my dear. [*Seizes her. The* **Sergt.** *seizes* **Bess.** *The girls scream for help.* **Ysobel** *draws revolver and points*

it at **Diaz,** *who holds* **Cora** *in front of him.*] Fire if you dare !
[*They carry or drag* **Cora** *and* **Bess** *off* L. U. E., *screaming.*]

Hut. [*Running on* R. 2 E.] What's the matter ? [*Soldiers follow* **Hutton** *on.*]

Yso. Diaz and his guerillas. They have abducted Cora and Bess, and have taken them that way. [*Pointing* L.]

Hut. Forward, men. [*Leads through gateway.*] Prepare to fire a volley. [*They load.*]

Yso. Stop ! You will kill the girls.

Hut. And they will thank me. Even death is better than the fate intended for them. Aim ! Fire ! [*Men fire.*] Forward ! Double ! [*They dash off* L. *as curtain descends.*]

CURTAIN.

ACT III.

[SCENE I.—*Headquarters of the guerillas. A hut in the mountains back of Santiago. At rise* **Lieut. Cristobal** *and two men are playing cards at table,* C. *Others lounging about.*]

Lieut. C. [C., *behind table.*] What a reckless devil our captain is. Anything from cold victuals to money is plunder for him, and now he's taken to stealing girls. They're two mighty pretty girls, but they're not worth three men's lives. Besides, these pig Yankees have such queer ideas about women that they'll never·rest till they've been here to look for them.

Diaz. [*Who has appeared outside window and listened.*] You think so, eh ? Well, that's just what I want. [*Enters door in flat.*] My pretty Cora refused me when I offered to marry her. Very well. She'll never get another chance to be Mrs. Diaz. I have scores to settle with her and her lover, too, and all I ask is to entice him up here and make him my prisoner. Remember, boys, a hundred dollars to the man who takes Captain Hutton alive. [*Men shout.*]

Lieut. C. He'll not be such a fool as to venture here alone. [*Who has risen. Comes down with* **Diaz.**]

Diaz. Don't be too sure. For her sake he'll venture anything, and I have arranged a trap into which he is very apt to tumble. How is *your* sweetheart this morning ?

Lieut. C. She's a perfect little devil. I tried to kiss her and she clawed my face like a wildcat. [*Points to scratched face patched with court plaster.*] I think I'll turn her over to San‑chez, here. He has a playful way of knocking a woman down when she doesn't obey orders. I'm too tender-hearted with the fair sex.

Diaz. I haven't had time to bring my charmer to terms, but she'll have to give in, sooner or later. Have any of the missing men turned up yet ?

Lieut. C. No. Not one of them.

Diaz. Then they must have been killed when Hutton fired that volley. Alvarez, Garno and Caragua—three good men, and they shall be avenged. Well, clear out now, all of you. I'm going to make love to my American beauty. [*The men laugh boisterously and ex. door in flat, taking guns from rack against* C. *flat as they go. Three guns, with fixed bayonets, are left in rack.*]

Lieut. C. Here's the key, Captain. [*Hands key.*] Now, play fair—don't meddle with my little spitfire.

Diaz. Don't be alarmed. I'll have my hands full with my own. Now ambush your men, so as to command the narrow pass, and keep strict watch. If a lone man or woman approaches, don't show yourselves. Should Hutton or anybody else come with soldiers, wait till they are well into the pass, and then pick them off at your ease when they are surrounded.

L'eut. C. How about the upper pass ?

Diaz. That is known only to us, and no outsider could find it without a guide. Now, keep your men out of sight, obey orders strictly, and we'll have Oscar Hutton in a trap very soon from which he'll never escape.   .

Lieut. C. What a position this mountain would be for the Americanos ! With a battery of big guns they could destroy Cervera's fleet and bombard Santiago at their leisure.   .

Diaz. They'd never attempt to drag heavy ordnance up these heights, which are already occupied by Gen. Linares. Now, be off. [**Lieut. C.** *salutes and exits door in flat.* **Diaz** *watches through window.*]

Lieut. C. [*Outside.*] Fall in. Fall in there. Right face. Forward—march. [*They pass window.*]

Diaz. They're off. Now for Cora. [*Unlocks door,* R. 2 E.] Well, my little birds, is your cage becoming uncomfortably small ?

Bess. [*Appearing at door.*] It's so small that there's no room in here for you. [*Slams door in his face.*]

Diaz. [*Pushes door open after some trouble.*] You would, eh? I've a good mind to kiss you for that. [**Bess** *shoves a broom at him, he jumps back. She stands at door.*]

Bess. Take my advice, and have a better mind not to. Your sergeant tried it this morning and you ought to see his face.

Diaz. I've seen it, but I'm not afraid of a little scratchcat.

Bess. Are you going to let us out of here?

Diaz. I'm going to let Cora out. You'll have to stay there till you get better tempered. Come out, Cora.

Cora. [*Within.*] Not one step.

Diaz. We'll see about that. [*Enters room and flings **Cora** out.*]

Cora. You coward!

Bess. [*Slipping out behind him.*] Don't call him that, Cora, you're too complimentary. Listen to me. You *Spaniard*.

Diaz. Get back in there. Do you hear me? Get back in there.

Bess. [*Keeping the table between them.*] What for?

Diaz. Because I tell you to.

Bess. That's a mighty good reason for not doing it.

Diaz. I've had enough of this fooling. [*Rushes at her, catches her and forces her into room. Locks door, leaving key in it.*] Now stay there.

Cora. What a heartless brute you are! [*In front of table.*]

Diaz. [R. C.] Who made me what I am? You. Why did I take desperate risks in order to become rich? So that I might win you. When the market turned against me and all was lost—every dollar I had schemed and toiled for gone—who showed me the way to secure funds and continue the game? You.

Cora. I? How? When? [**Ysobel** *appears at window.*]

Diaz. The day you came to the bank and confided to me the fact that your brother was short in his accounts. You asked me to ascertain the amount so that you might save him from disgrace, and you then showed me how I could obtain $50,000 with the certainty of throwing the blame on him if the money was lost in the stock market.

Cora. Absurd! Why should I suggest such a thing?

Diaz. There was no need. It suggested itself. Phillip was

already an embezzler. Why not a forger, too ? I simply varied
my signature slightly on a number of checks, sent him to draw
the money, and denied the checks when they came in from the
banks. See—here is a complete record of the whole transaction. [*Opens table drawer and shows memorandum-book.
Pitches it back and closes the drawer. Drawer is up stage.
While his back is turned* **Ysobel** *gets through window.*]

Cora. [*Down* R. C.] I suppose it was also I who made you
a traitor to the land you lived in, a spy for the government of
Spain. [*Crosses to* L. C. **Ysobel** *hides behind blanket screen-
ing* R. *upper corner.*]

Diaz. [*Sits on* R. *lower corner of table.*] A secret service
agent is a spy or a patriot, according to whose side he is on.
I call myself a patriot. You call me a spy. My country re-
wards me. Yours would hang me. [*He is seated on table.*
Ysobel *comes out of her hiding-place, makes a gesture for
silence to* **Cora,** *who is* L. C. *and sees her, sneaks down, opens
drawer and secures memo-book. She holds it up so that audience can see it ; then goes to door,* R. 2 E., *unlocks it and
lets* **Bess** *out, keeping the key. She then goes to stand of arms,
gives* **Bess** *a gun and brings the other two down behind table.
This is done during the speeches which follow,* **Cora** *assisting
by keeping* **Diaz** *watching her down* L. C.]

Cora. My country *will* hang you unless you are killed before
you are captured.

Diaz. I am taking my chance of that. But suppose we talk
of something more pleasant. Do you know what I intend to
do with you ?

Cora. What you intend to do matters little. Your intentions are doubtless as vile as your wicked imagination can suggest, but you shall never carry them out.

Diaz. Who will prevent me ?

Cora. My friend, and myself.

Diaz. Don't talk nonsense. You are alone here with me.
I am a man—you, a woman. I am strong—you are weak. No
power on earth can protect you.

Cora. But there is a power in heaven that can.

Diaz. [*Laughs.*] When it comes to a test between the
powers of heaven and the powers of the other place, the other
place seems to triumph about nine times out of ten.

Cora. It will not triumph this time.

Diaz. Your courage is superb. I can't help admiring the
way you defy me.

Cora. I don't fear you. In spite of your sneers I believe that the power you pretend to despise will protect the innocent and punish the guilty.

Diaz. If you had loved instead of hating me you might have taught me to believe that, too. As it is, I love you, in spite of your bitter scorn, and one of these days you are going to love me.

Cora. Not while I live.

Diaz. [*Reaches chair* L. *of table and sits down.*] Come here and sit on my knee. [*By this time* **Bess** *and* **Ysobel** *are* L. C. *just behind table, with the guns.*]

Cora. I'll not !

Diaz. Then I'll make you. [*As he steps down stage toward her she darts up.* **Ysobel** *gives her gun. As* **Diaz** *turns the three girls bring the guns to the charge. Picture.*]

Cora. Advance one step and we will kill you.

Diaz. José—Sancho—Juan. [*Calling.*]

Yso. Keep your eyes on *him.* This is a trick to throw us off our guard. His men are *not* here. [*They don't look around. Door* L. 3 E. *opens and three men steal down behind them.*]

Diaz. [C.] Ah, Señora—your Spanish blood renders you proof against Spanish strategy.

Yso. At least against so simple a ruse as that. Back up to the door, girls. [*They do so.*]

Diaz. [*Seeing that his men are ready.*] Now ! [*Each man disarms a girl and throws her to her knees, threatening her with bayonet.* **Diaz** *laughs.*] What did I tell you ? Who triumphs now ? Back, men, but be ready to answer a call. [*Men ex. door,* L. 3 E., *taking guns with them.*] Now, you two young ladies will retire to that room. Miss Cora wishes to hold a private conversation with me. Resistance is useless, as you already know.

Yso. You triumph for the moment, but the end means defeat, disaster—death !

Bess. You wait till my Milton gets hold of you. He'll fix you for this ! [*They ex. into room,* R. 2 E. **Diaz** *closes door. He is unable to lock it because* **Ysobel** *removed the key when liberating* **Bess.** **Ysobel** *immediately gets out and exits through window, when he returns to* **Cora** *down* C., *in front of table.*]

Diaz. Now, my dear, I want a kiss, and I'm going to have it.

Cora. Stand back ! I warn you that I will fight as long as I am able.

Diaz. That won't be very long. [*Takes hold of her.* **Cora** *struggles and screams.* **Hutton** *enters door in flat, revolver in hand.*]

Hut. [*Pointing revolver.*] Let go! [**Bess** *appears at door,* R 2 E.]

Diaz. Trapped! [*Putting* **Cora** *between them so that* **Hutton** *will hit her if he fires.* **Hutton** *closes with* **Diaz**, *who grabs his wrist to prevent his use of revolver. Calls.*] José! Quick! [*The three men rush in, disarm* **Hutton** *and hold him,* L. C. **Cora** *faints over table.*] Well done, boys! [*Raises* **Cora** *in his arms.*] Now, Oscar Hutton, she is mine, and you are at my mercy. Nothing stands between me and my revenge.

Yso. [*Suddenly appearing at window.*] You're wrong, Fernando Diaz—*I* do!

[CHANGE TO SCENE 2.]

[SCENE 2.—*A tropical wood in first grooves. Log on* L. *to sit on. At change* **Dr. H. Bev.** *and* **Corny**, *armed with guns, enter* L. I E.]

Dr. H. · [C.] This is where Miss Carlos told us to wait for her. We are within half a mile of the guerillas' headquarters.

Corny. [R.] Thin I am hanged if I like the place. Oh, if I was only back in Washington, minglin' wid the great min of me nation in the halls of Congress!

Bev. [L. *Laughs.*] *I* nevah saw yo do much minglin', 'cept wid de hosses and mules in de halls of ol' Mars Walton's barn.

Corny. [*Throws down gun.*] Oh, if I ever kick him in the shins! Don't tempt me, naygur—'tis all I can do to kape me boots off ye now.

Bev. Yo' kick me in de shins—yo' des try it, Irish—I's a Darktown Cubian, I is, an' I carries a razzor. [*Shows razor.*] Zizz! Zizz! [*Slashing.*]

Dr. H. Give me that weapon. [*Takes it from him.*] Give it up, sir.

Bev. Well, now, gimme a squar deal. Take off dat Irishman's shoes, so he cain't kick.

Corny. An' lave me to get butted to death wid that ironclad skull of yours? Get out, ye black billygoat.

Dr. H. Stop it. Both of you. This is no time for quarrelling. Two of the dearest girls in the world are in deadly peril.

Their friends should have but one quarrel now, and that with the scoundrels who carried them off. You ought to be ashamed of yourselves.

Corny. Thrue for you, Docthor. [*Aside.*] That coon 'ud provoke a saint.

Bev. Dat's a fact. [*Aside.*] If I evah carve dat Irishman I'll cut to de bone.

Dr. H. Now shake hands, and behave yourselves. [*They advance reluctantly,* **Beverly** *showing more willingness than* **Corny.**] Go on, Corny—shake hands, or I'll make you *kiss* him.

Corny. [*Aside.*] Howly mother ! Talk about takin' a black draft ! [*Shakes hands.*]

Dr. H. Now, Corny, you let Beverly alone from this time on.

Corny. I won't say another word. I won't even look at him, bedad ! [*Goes* R. *and takes up gun.*]

Bev. Dat's all I ask. Keep yo' head shet, an' yo' mouf shet, an' yo' eyes shet, an' yo' ears shet, an' den yo' keep out o' trouble wid me.

Dr. H. Now, if you two think you can agree for about five minutes, I'll climb that little hill [*Pointing* R.], and see if she is coming. While I'm gone you sit down over there, Beverly, and you, Corny, act as sentry. That'll keep you apart. [*Ex.* R. I E.]

Bev. Say, Irish, I was only foolin'. [*Sitting on log,* L.]

Corny. [*Marching back and forth.*] Well, don't fool wid me that way ag'in, for you're liable to get hurted, me bould bucko. Sure this climate is enough to sour the milk of human kindness in any white man. [*Wiping off perspiration.*]

Bev. Dat's a fact, or black man either. [*Fanning himself with hat.*]

Corny. Begorra, I don't enjoy the rations round here, at all, at all.

Bev. Rations ? What rations ?

Corny. Perspirations, ye brunette beauty. I wisht I had a good, long drink. I'm as dry as dust.

Bev. Dust ! Dat's what we's all made of, Corny. De Lawd took dust and made Adam.

Corny. Well, whin He made *you* He must have tuk coal dust.

Bev. Dat's all right. Dey *sells* coal dust, 'cause it's worth something ; but yo' common, ordinary, *white* dust—dey des sprinkles water on it till its name is mud, an' den dey scrapes it up and frows it on de dump heap.

Corny. Listen to the talkin' machine ! Did ye bring ere a sup wid you, I dunno ?

Bev. Not a drop. But, say, Corny—how would a nice, big slice of watahmillion strike you' ? Watahmillion on ice.

Corny. Wathermelon ! On ice ! Oh, ye tantalizer-—an' me wid the tongue of me hangin' out ! Begorra, I've often wondered how the divil all that wather gets into the melons, Beverly.

Bev. Well, fo' de Lawd's sake, doesn't yo' know dat ?

Corny. No, I don't, an' no more do you.

Bev. 'Deed I does. Dey always plants watahmillions in de spring.

Corny. Sure I know that, but where does the wather come from ?

Bev. Why, from de *spring*, of co'se.

Corny. From the spring ! Go 'long, you black nigger-amus.

Bev. Say, Corny, does yo' 'spec' dey's any of dem guerillers roun' heah ?

Corny. Well, I hope not—for your swate sake.

Bev. Whaffo' do yo' suppose dey calls um guerillers ?

Corny. Well, ye poor ignorant black divil, listen an' I'll explain it to ye. A guerilla, d'ye moind, is a monkey—the biggest ape in the world, an' they call these fellys guerillas because ivery toime our gallant byes come forninst thim they make a monkey of thim.

Bev. [*Laughs.*] Sho' 'nuff, Corny, sho' 'nuff. Make a monkey of dem—dat's good. [*Laughs.*]

Corny. Say, Bev—ye wor pretty flip about Adam an' the dust a few minutes ago. Do you know your Bible ?

Bev. 'Deed I does—from Genesee to de Revolutions.

Corny. An' what church do you belong to ?

Bev. I's a Baptis', I is.

Corny. That 'ud never do me. Too much wather. Besides, they're too new. I belave in the ould, ancient religion.

Bev. Cain't be no mo' older nor ancienter dan de Baptis'. No, sah. Dat's what I remarked. Why, de Baptises is mentioned in de Scriptures. Yes, sah.

Corny. Ah, go 'long—you're off your riservation.

Bev. I'll done prove it. Yo' search de good book, but yo' don't find nuffin' 'bout James, de Mefodis, or Thomas, de 'piscalopian, or Sandy, de Presbyterium—but yo' does find about John, de Baptis'. Yes sah !

Corny. Well, now, tell me, seein' you know so much—who made the monkey ?

Bev. Dat's easy. De same one made de monkey what made de Irish.

Corny. I'll bate the divil out of you for that. [*Threatening him with clubbed gun.*]

Bev. [*On his knees.*] Hol' on—hol' on—let me finish. De same one made de black man too.

Corny. That saved your life. But don't thry me too far— me timper won't stand much in this heat. [*Goes* R.]

Bev. I won't say another word. [*Starts singing.* **Corny** *paces back and forth till he can't stand it any longer.*]

Corny. Shut up, will ye ? Shut up ! I can stand no more of your blamed noise.

Bev. I wasn't singin' fo' yo' amusement. No, sah ! I sings to please myself.

Corny. Thin you're mighty aisy plazed.

Dr. H. [*Off* R.] Hello—o—o ! [*At a distance.*]

Bev. Oh, Lord ! dem monkeys ! I mean guerillers. [*Frightened,* L.]

Dr. H. [*Off* R.] Hello—o—o—o !

Corny. 'Tis the Docthor, ye chocolate crame. Hello ! Sure there's Miss Carlos wid him. Come on, he's beckonin' us. [*Grabs* **Bev.** *and puts him in front,* R.]

Bev. [*After looking off* R.] Is—is yo' sho' it ain't dem Spaniels tryin' to fool us ?

Corny. [*Prodding him with gun from behind.*] Go on— you an' your monkeys an' Spaniels. Forward—march. [*Prodding him as they march off* R. 1 E.]

[SCENE 3.—*A mountain pass in the Sierra Cobre. Rock wings and sky borders. Barricade built of logs, lumber, boxes and barrels. The platforms must be strong. At rise,* **Diaz** *discovered seated* R. C. *on box.* **Lieut. C.** *standing before him. Guerillas lounging about. One man on platform* R., *as lookout. Box used as table has small American flag on it covered with papers, writing material, maps, etc.* **Diaz** *is studying a map.*]

Diaz. I tell you, Cristobal, we can hold this position against an army.

Lieut. C. Against infantry, yes. But suppose they bring a battery of field guns up the mountain and begin shelling us, how long would that flimsy barricade stand ?

Diaz. Not very long. But there is no likelihood of that. In his eagerness to reach Santiago, Shalter will try to carry it by storm and not by siege. If he is not going to besiege he will not drag cannon up these difficult heights.

Lieut. C. This pass is one of the most important of all, for the heights above us command both city and harbor.

Diaz. And for that reason we must hold it at all hazards until reinforcements arrive from General Linares or General Pando.

Lieut. C. There is another thing. Suppose some of these Cuban dogs show the Yankees the way through the upper pass, and they attack us from above ?

Diaz. Señor Cristobal, if I hadn't seen you under fire I should call you a coward. As it is, I merely say you indulge too many fears.

Lieut. C. Señor Capitan, war, with me, is a trade which I have followed from boyhood. With you it is a novelty, and longer experience will teach you greater caution.

Diaz. Don't lecture me, Señor Lieutenant—I won't stand it. Now, by way of amusing ourselves, bring Hutton before me. [**Lieut. C.** *salutes and ex.* L. 2 E.] I don't like that fellow. He has too many opinions of his own, and it wouldn't surprise me if he gets shot in the back during our next fight. His influence with the men is growing too strong, anyway, for perfect discipline. [**Lieut. C.** *re-enters with* **Hutton,** *who is in his shirt-sleeves, blindfolded and with his arms tied together behind him.* **Lieut. C.** *removes the blind.*] Now, Captain, I hope you are quite comfortable. [*Pause.*] Why don't you answer ?

Hut. [C.] You didn't ask me a question. [**Lieut. C.** *is* L. C. *Men grouped across stage.*]

Diaz. In the old days, in Washington, you were always ready enough with your tongue. In fact, you were about the greatest braggart I ever knew.

Hut. Diaz, you lie. [*Quietly.*]

Diaz. I what ? [*Starting to his feet, goes to him.*] What did you say ?

Hut. You lie. I never brag.

Diaz. [*Slaps his face.*] Take that. You remember, I owe it to you. [*Guerillas mutter " Shame ! "*]

Hut. You coward ! When I struck *you* your hands were free, and I was ready and anxious to give you whatever satisfaction you might demand. You strike me when I am bound and helpless.

Diaz. [*Sitting down* R. C.] You followed up that contemptuous slap in the face by putting a bullet in my body. That is another debt which I intend to pay—with interest. You gave me one bullet, I'll give you five.

Hut. Call it by its right name. You intend to murder me.

Diaz. Oh, no—I'm going to try you by court-martial and abide by the sentence of the court.

Hut. If you're a man you will free my hands and fight me. Take any weapon you choose and give me the chance for *my* life that I gave you for yours. If you persist in doing what you threaten, you are a cowardly assassin, and my murder will be fully avenged by my fellow-countrymen.

Diaz. Your rabble of thieves and pickpockets, which you call an army, was defeated and hurled back by General Linares in yesterday's battle. To-day your Yankee friends will be driven into the sea. [*Distant cannon shot heard.*] Hark— what's that ?

Hut. That is the bark of a Yankee bulldog which gives the lie to the falsehood you have just uttered. [*Cannon heard.*] Do you hear it ? The battle of Santiago has been resumed, and when it is finished the Stars and Stripes will fly from your citadel to tell the world that another pledge has been given to freedom, another tyrant has been laid low.

Diaz. Fool ! Do you know that you are in my power, that you stand face to face with death ?

Hut. I know it. I am an American soldier and not afraid to die.

Diaz. Then I'll make you afraid. I'll show you something that will wring your heart. [*Calling.*] Lieutenant, bring my pretty prisoner here.

Lieut. C. Señor Capitan, I'd like to suggest—— [*Cannon heard.*]

Diaz. Don't you suggest anything. Obey my orders. [*Ex. Lieut.,* R. 2 E.] It may ease your dying moments to know that your ladylove will be left in better hands than yours, Captain.

Hut. What ! You have dared to drag that gentle girl to this wild place ? Oh, Heaven ! If I were only free for five short minutes, and alone with you, I'd march to meet death with a smile.

Diaz. And what would make you so happy, Captain ?

Hut. [L. C.] The knowledge that she was free from so foul a thing as you, forever.

Diaz. [*Rises. He has remained seated until now.*] Oh,

well, you're not free and you never will be until you get your freedom in another world. [*Lieut. C. re-enters with* **Cora.** **Bess** *follows.*]

Co:a.   Oscar! [*About to embrace him. Cannon heard.*]

Diaz.   [*Stopping her.*] Wait! Before you greet that gentleman I have something to say to you. [*Lieut. C. goes up, where he watches scene with men.*]

Cora.   Well, sir?

Diaz.   [C.] Our mutual friend, Captain Hutton, has rendered himself very obnoxious to the Spanish government by acting as a spy for the Yankee forces.

Cora.   [R. C.] That is not true. Captain Hutton is not a spy.

Bess.   [R.] No! Captain Hutton is an officer and a gentleman.

Diaz.   He was captured while making a reconnaissance of our position, which is now of the utmost importance to the enemy. He *is* a spy, and as such he will be dealt with. [*Sits R. C.*]

Hut.   This is infamous! I followed a band of ruffians who had abducted two hospital nurses from a house protected by the red cross of humanity. Those ruffians wore no uniform to distinguish them as members of the Spanish army. I, on the other hand, wore the uniform of mine. I traced them to their retreat and, while trying to rescue one of the two kidnapped women, was made a prisoner.

Diaz.   You hear, men? He cal's you a band of ruffians—says that you do not belong to the Spanish army—*he* says this, the Yankee spy who came here for the purpose of guiding the pigs through this pass to kill you. [*The men growl threateningly.*]

Lieut. C.   It ought to be considered that he is this lady's lover, and——

Diaz.   Silence! Nothing should be considered but the evidence which you have heard. You all have your own opinions formed, but I will give the prisoner the benefit of every voice by appointing you all a court-martial to render judgment. Is he guilty or not guilty?

Lieut. C.   First let us hear the evidence. [*Coming down to L. C.*]

Diaz.   It has all been heard. I now demand a verdict.

Lieut. C.   This is not in accordance with military law, nor with the customs of civilized warfare, so I refuse to act as a

member of any such court. [*Crosses* L. *and sits down on box.
All but four of the guerillas follow him and group* L.]

Diaz. [*Aside*]. Curse him ! But I'll not be balked ! [*Aloud.*]
Very well. All are excused except José, Sancho, Juan and
Monte. Is the prisoner, accused of being a spy, guilty or not
guilty ? [*These four men have remained* C.]

Four men. Guilty.

Diaz. A just verdict. And the punishment ?

Four men. Death. [**Bess** *crosses to* **Lieut. C.** *and pantomimes a conversation.*]

Diaz. And a just punishment. I confirm the sentence.
Prisoner, you have heard the verdict, have you anything to say
before the sentence is carried into effect ?

Hut. Nothing, except that you are a deliberate murderer.
Even your men are ashamed of such a butchery. [*With a
gesture toward* **Lieut. C.,** L.]

Diaz. [*Rises.*] The sentence shall be executed forthwith.
Lieutenant Cristobal, select a firing party, place the prisoner
against the barricade and shoot him. [**Lieut.** *does not move.*]
Did you hear my order ?

Lieut. C. [*Rises and salutes.*] I did, Señor Capitan. [*Advancing to* C.]

Diaz. Obey at once, or I'll try you for mutiny.

Lieut. C. Señor Capitan, this is a mockery of justice. Your
order is unlawful and I'll die rather than obey it. [*Salutes.*]

Diaz. [*Strips the red and yellow sash off* **Lieut. C.**] Your
sword. [**Lieut. C.** *unbuckles sword, hands it with left hand,
drawing revolver with right hand.*] What do you mean by
that ?

Lieut. C. That is merely a precaution in case of treachery.

Diaz. You are under arrest. I'll deal with you presently.
[*Hands sword to* **Jose,** *puts sash over his shoulder.*] José,
you are appointed acting-lieutenant in place of Cristobal, reduced
to the ranks. Take charge of this execution. [*Sits down.*
Jose *motions to* **Sancho, Juan** *and* **Monte,** *who take charge of*
Hutton. Lieut. C. *joins the men* L. **Bess** *crosses* R. *to* **Cora.**]

Jose. Forward—march ! [*They march* **Hutton** *up stage,
blindfold him, and make him kneel. Then they march down*
L. C.] Halt ! about face. Prepare to fire a volley.

Cora. [*Screams.*] Mercy ! mercy ! You cannot— you will
not murder him before my eyes. In heaven's name—I beg you
on my knees—order them to stop. [*Kneeling.* **Bess** *is crying,* R.]

Diaz. On certain conditions.

Cora. Name them.

Diaz. I will free him and guarantee him safe escort, blindfolded, from this place to Shafter's lines, provided he will trample this rag, the Stars and Stripes, underfoot, and drink the health of the King of Spain. [*Rises, holding small American flag.*]

Hut. [*Rises.*] Never! I'd rather die the most ignominious death than act the traitor to that glorious flag.

Cra. Shoot me if you will—but don't insult my country's emblem. [*Snatches flag from him.*]

Diaz. Then I have one other proposal. If you love this man, Cora, you alone can save him.

Cora. How?

Diaz. Remain here with me, of your own free will—be mine —and I give you his life. If you love him better than yourself you will consent.

Hut. Don't answer him! Treat his infamous proposal with the silent scorn it merits.

Cora. [*Goes quickly up stage, flings her arms and the flag around* **Hut.** *The firing party is by this time down stage.*] Men—you have mothers, sisters, sweethearts. Remember them. In the name of the women you love, save me from far worse than death! Let me die with him. See—I am not afraid. I need no blindfold. I, myself, will give the word and you shall see how an American girl can die.

Diaz. [*Aside.*] She dare not do it. This is a trick to move my sympathy. [*Aloud.*] Let her have her own way—if she wants to die, she may. [**Cora** *embraces* **Hutton,** *who is standing, and whispers to him. He kisses her.* **Bess** *takes a silent farewell, crying, and goes down* L. *to* **Lieut. C.**]

Cora. [*Kneels with* **H.** *Folds hands in prayer. Then with her arms around* **Hutton.**] I am ready. Load. [*The soldiers obey orders.*] Aim. [*They aim.*]

Lieut. C. Stop! [*Followed by his men rushes between the firing party and the two prisoners.*] This infamy shall not go on! I'm a soldier, not a hyena, nor a murderer. I'm willing to die for Spain, but not to see a woman assassinated.

Diaz. This is mutiny.

Lieut. C. Call it what you like. I and the men who back me are ready to answer to the general commanding for what we do, and we shall see to it that this man and woman are taken before him for a proper hearing.

Diaz. You'll be shot for this.

Man. [*Lookout on rocks*, R.] Flag of truce.

Diaz. Where? [*Goes up ladder and looks off* R.] A wounded man, bearing a flag of truce? Halt, there! Two of you go and blindfold him and lead him over the rocks. [*Two guerillas go over rocks* R. *and disappear.*] Where are you from? [**Lieut. C.** *takes bandage off* **Hutton's** *eyes.*]

Phil. [*Off at back.*] General Lawton, with a proposal for exchange.

Diaz. Bring him in. [*The men lead* **Phil.** *over rock. His head is bandaged and his arm is in a sling. His eyes are blindfolded.*]

Phil. [*After being led down stage.*] Where is the commandant?

Diaz. I am he.

Phil. Diaz! I know your voice.

Diaz. [*Pulls the bandage off his eyes.*] Phillip Walton!

Cora. Phillip! [**Cora, Bess** *and* **Hutton** *come down and greet him.*]

Diaz. [R. C.] Stand back! [*They retire* L.] Why have you come here under a flag of truce?

Phil. [C.] General Lawton sent me with a proposal to exchange three men of your command, captured last night—Alvarez, Garno and Caragua—for Captain Hutton. This is according to the recognized cartel—three privates for one captain. General Lawton also demands the immediate and unconditional surrender of my sisters, who, as hospital nurses and non-combatants, are exempt from such molestation.

Diaz. Major-generals do not send such messages by private soldiers. You are an impostor.

Phil. I am a lieutenant in the army of the United States, promoted on the field yesterday. [*Shows shoulder-strap.*]

Cora. For bravery! My brother! [**Lieut. C., Hutton, Cora** *and* **Bess** *are* L. C.]

Phil. Well—a lucky accident, at any rate, which General Lawton happened to notice.

Diaz. And if I refuse to make the exchange, or surrender the nurses?

Phil. In that case General Lawton will hold you personally responsible for the safety of all three, and will be here in a few minutes to take them out of your hands.

Diaz. Men, will you fight for the honor of your flag if I guarantee that the prisoners shall all be taken before General Torral?

4

Lieut. C. We will. [*Men shout. They carry off the boxes* R. C. *and* L.]

Diaz. Then, Cristobal, I restore your rank. See that the prisoners are kept in safety until we have repelled this attack. As for you, Phillip Walton, you must remain here. You have seen my strength and my defences.

Phil. Much obliged. I wished to remain for the protection of my sisters.

Diaz. [*To* **Lieut. C.**] Put them under guard in the cavern there and tell your men to shoot either of them who tries to escape.

Lieut. C. [*Salutes.*] Your order shall be obeyed. José. [*Takes sash and sword, putting them on.*] Sancho. You two will guard the prisoners with your lives. [*They march* **Cora, Bess, Hutton** *and* **Phillip** *off* R. 2 E.]

Look out. [*On rocks,* R.] The enemy.

Diaz. [*Goes up ladder. Looks off.*] They are descending from the upper pass! We've been betrayed! Up, men, and give them a reception! [*Men go up ladders* R. *and* L.] There they come. Fire! [*Guerillas fire. Answering shots are fired off.*] Pick them off as they advance. [*Men fire independently.* **Diaz** *catches a wounded man and helps him down. Others are wounded and leap or scramble down ladders* **Diaz** *goes to* R. 2 E. *and calls.*] José, Cristobal. [*They enter.*] Let the women attend our wounded if they will. [*José exits.* **Lieut. C.** *goes up and directs men firing. They carry the wounded down to* R. 2 E. **Cora** *and* **Bess** *bandage heads, legs and arms.*]

D'az. [*To* **Cora.**] I didn't think you would do this for your enemies,

Cora. The Red Cross knows neither friends nor enemies. We aid all who suffer. [**Hutton** *enters* R. 2 E. *with his arms free. The firing continues both on and off.*]

Diaz. [*Seeing him.*] Not yet. [*Fires revolver at* **Hutton,** *who sinks into* **Cora's** *arms.*]

Cora. Murderer! [*She and* **Bess** *attend* **Hutton,** *who appears to be dead. Cannon have been heard close by. A big explosion occurs outside the barricade, which tumbles in as if a shell had struck it. Cheer heard off.*]

Diaz. There's only one way of escape, men. Follow me! [*Guerillas jump from rocks* R. *and* L. *as American soldiers, led by* **Lieut. Fisk,** *with bayonets fixed and cheering, enter* C. **Diaz** *rushes to* L. 2 E., *followed by Spaniards, but is met by*

Merry, *who enters with his sailors. Spaniards throw down their guns and kneel* C. *imploring mercy in dumb show.* **Lieut. Cristobal** *is offering his sword to* **Fisk. Merry** *has his sword against* **Diaz's** *chest.*

CURTAIN.

ACT IV.

[SCENE I.—*An apartment in the Hotel Tacon, Santiago de Cuba. Fancy chamber with centre opening, curtained. Lighted lamp on table. Second-class furniture. Hotel private sitting-room. At rise of curtain,* **Cora,** *in blue, and* **Ysobel,** *in red evening dress, discovered on balcony. They, enter through centre opening and come down* C.]

Cora. Well, dear, this is a happy day for all of us, and our gallant boys have covered themselves with glory. The fall of Santiago will be remembered as long as the English language lasts. [*Cheers and shouts heard off in distance.*]

Yso. Not only are you Americans, and we Cubans, glad, but listen to the citizens. How they are cheering the regiments as they march into the town! Seven out of every ten were hoping for an American victory, but dared not betray their sentiments. [*Sits* R. *of table,* L. C.]

Cora. I think everybody rejoices except the official classes who have robbed the poor people for years, and have grown so rich out of their sufferings. But what has become of Phillip? He ought to rest, or he will get fever in that wound.

Yso. So I told him, but he refused to do so until he had succeeded in releasing my poor old father from his prison. I am so anxious, dear, for fear—for fear death may have released him already.

Cora. I trust not, Ysobel, most sincerely. I want to meet him and to tell him what a dear, fearless girl he has. [*Kisses her.*]

Yso. Don't, Cora. I don't deserve such praise.

Cora. If I stood on the balcony, there, and shouted your praises all day long, I couldn't do you justice. It was you who rescued me from the hands of that wretch in the mountain hut; you who guided our brave boys through that secret upper pass, and enabled them to defeat Diaz at the.moment he felt himself most secure.

Yso. Oh, psha ! Let's talk about something else. What do you think they'll do to Diaz ?

Cora. Take him back to Washington and try him for robbing the bank. Thanks to you, again, his own handwriting in that memorandum book will ensure his conviction. But where is Bess ? [**Bess** *heard singing " Three Cheers for the Red, White and Blue " off* L.]

Yso. Listen. There she is now. [*They open door* L. 2 E. **Bess** *enters, in white evening dress, with American flag over her shoulder. She marches around until she has finished the stanza.*] Why, Bess, what are you going to do ?

Bess. [*Up at steps.*] I've just discovered that the proprietor of this hotel is the bitterest, meanest, measliest old Spaniard in town, and I'm going to show my colors and give him a pain in the back of his neck—you see if I don't.

Bev. [*Enters door* L. 2 E. *with hammer and nails.*] Heah dey is, Missy. I done got um at last, but I mos' had to lick dat ol' Spaniel to do it.

Bess. Come right along and nail it up good and tight. If old Sancho—Pedro—High—Low—Jack—and the Game, or whatever his name is, tries to haul down that flag he'll be in more trouble than Linares, Torral and Cervera all rolled into one. [*Goes out on balcony followed by* **Bev.** *They nail flag, upright, to balustrade. Great cheering heard outside as soon as the flag is seen.*]

Cora. [*Up stage.* **Ysobel** *with her.*] Listen to them ! You could almost imagine yourself at a flag-raising at home on the 4th of July.

Yso. From this time forward, I hope, the 4th of July will be the greatest holiday in the year from one end of Cuba to the other. The proudest destiny my country can achieve is to become another star in the azure field of your Old Glory.

Phil. [*Enters door* L. 2 E., *with* **Antonio Carlos**. *a ragged old man, with white hair and beard very much like Rip Van Winkle after his long sleep.*] Ysobel. [*As they go* C.]

.Yso. Phillip ! [*Going to him. Draws back, horror-stricken.*]

Carlos. [C.] My child. [*He is very feeble. Stretching out his hands.*]

Yso. Merciful heaven ! Can this be my father ?

Carlos. [*Sadly.*] It is the wreck of Antonio Carlos.—

Starved, half-mad with cruel treatment and anxiety, beaten and abused—I am still a living and a bitter testimony against Spanish misrule in my beloved Cuba.

Yso. [*Caressing him.*] My poor, poor father! Thank Heaven we have found you still alive. [*Seats him on sofa,* R. **Cora** *and* **Bess** *up* C.   **Phil.,** R. C. ; **Bev.,** *down* L.]

Carlos. Some died—many were murdered—but I lived on to see my child again.

Bev. [*Aside.*] If young Mars Phillip done get his way, reckon de ol' man gwan ter see his gran'chilluns, too.

Yso. These are my dearest friends, father—Miss Bassett and Miss Walton.

Bess. [*As he tries to rise.*] No, no, don't get up, Señor, I beg. You are weak and ill.

Carlos. [*Rising.*] A Cuban gentleman, Señora, must be ill indeed when he fails in his tribute to youth, beauty and those his daughter loves. [*Kisses their hands with stately politeness. To* **Cora.**] So you are the sister of the young Señor Lieutenant who sought me in that living tomb, and brought me forth to breathe once more the breath of freedom. [**Bess** *and* **Ysobel** *bring an arm-chair from up stage.*]

Cora. Yes, Phillip is my brother, Señor.

Carlos. Happy brother to have such a sister—happy sister to possess a brother who has shed his blood that tyranny might die and freedom live. [*Sits in arm-chair. They place pillows, footstools, etc., for him.*]

Bev. [*Aside to* **Phil.**] Mars Phil—Mars Phil—dar's yo' chance. Hit him while he's feelin' good to'ds yo'.

Phil. [*Aside to* **Bev.**] You shut up, will you ? I haven't asked *her* yet.

Bev. Den yo's foolish. Golly ! I'd 'a' done that, 'way back yer in Washington las' winter, ef I was you. [*Band heard off in distance, coming closer, playing "Marching through Georgia." Distant cheering heard.* **Bess** *and* **Cora** *go out on balcony, followed by* **Bev.**]

Phil. That's our regiment. I know the peculiar swing they give that tune.

Yso. Phillip, have you told father yet ?

Phil. No, Ysobel, not yet. I hadn't the courage until you were with me.

Carlos. Say no more, my children. I already feel toward Señor Phillip as toward a son. [*Taking their hands to join them.* **Ysobel** *is* R. *and* **Phil.** L. *of his chair.*]

Yso. [*Withdrawing her hand, confused.*] Oh, father—not that—you have misunderstood. [*Kneels beside him.*]

Phil. Ysobel, let me confess the truth. Señor, I am not known here as Phillip Walton, but under an assumed name in consequence of—of—a crime—but a crime for which, God knows, I have tried to atone. I have loved Ysobel since first we met, but because of my one false step I never told her so.

Carlos. That was honorable, my son. And what says my Ysobel ?

Yso. I—I love him, father. [*Hides her head on* **Carlos'** *breast.*]

Carlos. [*Rises, raises* **Ysobel,** *and joins their hands.*] He has atoned with his blood. His fault is blotted out forever. [*Extends his hands in silent blessing.*] Now I must rest. [*Goes up stage slowly.* **Ysobel** *and* **Phil.** *kiss swiftly, then go up and conduct* **Carlos** *to door,* R. 3 E. *He exits. They go to* C. *as band passes balcony, followed by troops, ad. lib., band going away in the distance.*]

Bess. [*On balcony.*] See—look ! There is Milton. He's left the line—he's coming in ! [*Runs to door* L. 2 E. *and exits.*]

Bev. [*Aside, coming down.*] Reckon dey's gwine ter be one marriage in de fambly, anyhow, by the looks of things. Sho ! Dat boy Phillip must be crazy not to spring de proposition on dat ol' man befo' he gits his sto' clo'es on. He's feelin' good and humble in dem ol' rags, but we gits to feelin' right proudy, us Cubians does, when we's all fixed up an' togged out to kill. B'lieve dat boy wants assistance. Dat s what I b'lieve. [*Goes up.*] Mars Phillip. Oh, Mars Phil !

Phil. [*Coming down.*] What is it, Beverly ?

Bev. Say, Mars Phil , don't yo' s'pose I could sorter 'range dis yer mattah between you an' Miss Ysobel ?

Phil. How do you mean "arrange" it ?

Bev. Why, yo's dead gone on de gal, an' de gal's dead gone on yo', an' de ol' man he's dead gone on de bofe of you, but yo's all kinder skeered to say so. Now, sposin' I des nachelly tell Missy Ysobel dat yo' 'low she's de onliest honeysuckle in de hull gyarden of gals, an' den, if she 'lows yo's mos' de onliest young hero in de ahmy, I goes to de ol' man an' sorter, kinder brokes de ice wid him ?

Phil. You do it, and I'll break your neck.

Bev. Why, Mars Phil—why—whaffo' yo' talk laik dat fo' ?

Phil. Because it's all fixed, and everything's settled except naming the day.

Bev. No! Sho'? Done got it all fixed up in dis little minute?

Phil. That's what I did. Now you hush up about it. [*Goes up.*]

Bev. Well, if dat boy don't beat de debbil! [**Merry** *and* **Bess** *enter door.* L. 2 E.] Sarvent, Mars Milton, sarvent, sah.

Merry. Hello, Beverly, what's the news? [*Shaking hands.*]

Bev. Don't let on I tol' you, now—dey's gwine ter be a weddin' in de fambly. Yo' heah me, sah?—dat's what I remarked—a weddin'.

Merry. Of course there is. That's no news, eh, Bess? And we're not going to wait till we get home, either.

Bess. Oh, Milton—I never said so.

Merry. But you're going to. We'll just bring this little event off next Monday night, as sure as you're a foot high.

Bess. I object.

Merry. What's your objection?

Bess. Why do you want to wait so long? [*He puts his arm around her. They go up stage, laughing.*]

Bev. Well, bress de Lawd—dat's two of um. [**Hutton,** *with head bandaged, enters door* R. 2 E.] Why, Mars Hutton! How is yo', sah? How's yo' wound?

Hut. Nearly well. It stunned me, that was all. Where's Miss Cora?

Cora. [*Seeing him.*] Oscar! [*Comes down rapidly.*] Oh, I'm so glad!

Hut. Darling! [*They embrace and then go out on balcony.*]

Bev. [*Aside.*] An' dat's free of um! Well bress mah black Baptis' soul! Dis yer fambly gwine ter hab weddin's to loan out to dey friends! [**Corny** *enters door,* L. 2 E.] Hello, Irish.

Corny. Hello, Spanish licorish.

Bev. Don't yo' call me no Spaniel—I's a Cubian, sah, an' proud of it. Don't yo' call me no Spaniel.

Corny. Oh, I was only jokin', man dear.

Bev. Well, dat's no joke to call a 'spectable man a Spaniel, des times. No, sah—no joke at all. Dat's what I remarked. Yo' heah me?

Corny. Oh, I heard you. I'm not blind. Where's the Captain?

Bev. Out on de balcony, engaged wid Missy Cora in some mos' pahticulah business an' cain't be 'sturbed, nohow.

Corny. Well, I've got to see him at once. There's the divil to pay. [*Starts to go up.* **Bev.** *holds him.*]

Bev. Hol' on. De Capting done tol' me he'd break ebery bone in mah brack hide if I let him be 'sturbed fo' de nex' half hour, an' his time's not up. [*Aside.*] Dem lovyers not gwine ter be 'sturbed if *I* can help it.

Corny. I've got to see him, I tell you. Lave go me. [*Wrenches away but* **Bev.** *catches him again.*]

Bev. Hol' on! Say, when's yo' gwine ter git married, Irish?

Corny. Marry the divil. What would the likes of me want to get married for?

Bev. Oh, I don't know. Everybody's gittin' married— Missy Cora an' Mars Hutton, Missy Ysobel an' young Mars Phillip, Missy Bess an' young Mars Milton, an', by golly, I's gwine ter look out fo' a nice, 'spectable widder lady my own self.

Corny. [*Breaks away. Going up.*] Captain, where are yez?

Hut. [*Entering from balcony.*] What is it, Corny?

Corny. Sure, sir, there's the divil to pay an' no pitch hot. [*The others enter* C.]

Hut. [*Coming down.*] What has happened?

Corny. That villain, Diaz, broke away from his guards as they were takin' him to lock him up, an' Liftinant Fisk is nearly wild wid rage.

Hut. What has he done? [*This brings everybody well down, much interested.*]

Corny. Sint the entire company out to chase him, an' the byes arc on his track. They've caught sight of him twice, but he runs like a deer an' doubles like a fox. [*Shouts and clamor heard outside, coming closer.*]

Hut. I'll go at once and see if anything further can be done. I wouldn't have that scoundrel escape for ten thousand dollars. [*Going* L.]

Merry. [*As the clamor grows louder.*] Listen—a hue and cry coming down the street! [*Goes up toward steps, when* **Diaz** *climbs over the balcony and dashes into the room like a hunted animal. This brings him past* **Merry,** *who gets between him and* C. *opening.*]

Everybody. Diaz!

Diaz. [*Seeing* **Corny,** R. C., *and* **Hutton,** L.] You—and *you!* Stand back, for I'll sell my life as dearly as possible! [*Draws revolver as* **Hutton** *starts for him and starts backing* *up toward steps* C. **Merry** *springs on him and gets revolver, pointing it at him.* **Diaz** *dashes at door,* R. 3 E. **Carlos** *enters and points at him accusingly.* **Diaz** *recoils in horror.*] Santa Maria! The ghost of Antonio Carlos—who died in prison. [*Backing down stage, little by little, followed by* **Carlos** *still in the same attitude and gazing fixedly at him.*] Don't look at me with those terrible eyes—take them off—take them off. [*Shrieks and falls* C. *Clamor outside. Soldiers enter* C. *from balcony.*]

Hut. [L. C.] Here is your prisoner. [**Corny** *and soldiers pick him up.*]

Diaz. [*Recovering from his faint.*] Trapped! It is real—he is alive—curse him—curse you all. How I hate you!

Hut. Silence! Take him away, and see that he doesn't escape again.

Corny. If he gets away from *me*, I'll give him my blessin'. Here—hould out your fishts. [*Takes handcuffs from pocket.*] Sure I borryed thim from a jondarmy [*gendarme*] widout axin' his lave, be raison I can't talk Cubebs. But, begorra, I had a notion I'd fall in wid you before the night was over. [*Handcuffs him.*] There, ye divil, axin' the ladies' pardon. I only wisht I had another pair on your legs. Come on, Bev, till I trate you to a glass of ice wather on the stren'th of it. Forward—march. [*Exit* **Corny, Bev., Diaz** *and soldiers, door* L. 2 E.]

Cora. [C. *with* **Hutton.**] He's gone, dearest—the only jarring note in the music of to-day.

Bess. [*Seated* R. *of table,* L. C., *with* **Merry,** *hanging over her chair.*] Very well, then, if you're in such an awful hurry, and don't care whether I have a stitch of clothes to my back or not, let it be to-morrow and get it over.

Lieut. Fisk. [*Knocks outside and opens door,* L. 2 E.] Excuse me if I intrude, Captain, but they told me I'd find you here. Busy?

Hut. [*Glancing at* **Cora.**] Rather. What is it?

Lieut. Fisk. Come in, Lieutenant. [**Lieut. C.** *enters. Salutes.*] Lieutenant Cristobal tells me you promised him a parole.

Hut. I did. Come here, sir. [**Cristobal** *advances to* L. C.] I want to take the hand of a brave and honest man. [*Shakes hands.*]

Cora. And I, of an enemy who proved our truest friend. [*Shakes hands.*]

Hut. Is this the dawn of peace ? I hope so with all my heart. [**Carlos** *is seated in arm-chair*, R. C. **Ysobel** *sits on a stool at his feet and* **Phillip** *stands* L. *of his chair.* **Cora** *is* C. *with* **Hutton** *on her* R., *and* **Cristobal** *on her* L. **Bess** *sits* L. *of table, and* **Merry** *hangs over her chair.* **Fisk** *is at the door.* **Beverly** *enters from balcony. Soldiers follow him.*]

Bev. Oh, Mars Hutton, I couldn't stop um, sah. 'Deed I couldn't. Dey was bent on comin'.

Hut. Who ?

Bev. Why, de boys of yo' company, sah. Dey des nachelly boun' to drink de health of all de brides, sah. Dat Irishman done tol' um.

Hut. Come in, boys, and welcome. You'll never wish long life and happiness to three prettier, sweeter, truer girls in the world than those who typify to-night the red, white and blue. [*Soldiers cheer and enter. Band on balcony plays chorus of* "*Red, White and Blue,*" *and all sing it as curtain descends.*]

NEW PLAYS, 1897-98.

The First Kiss.
Comedy in One Act,
BY
MAURICE HAGEMAN.
Author "By Telephone," "A Crazy Idea," Etc.

One male, one female characters. Plays twenty minutes. Scene, a handsomely furnished room. Costumes, afternoon dress of to-day. This sketch presents an entirely new plot, with novel situations and business. The fun is continuous and the dialogue bright and refined. Price, 15 cents.

Bird's Island.
Drama in Four Acts,
BY
MRS. SALLIE F. TOLER.
Author of "Handicapped," Etc.

Five male (may be played with four), four female characters. One exterior, two interior scenes. Costumes, summer costumes of to-day. Plays two and one-half hours. This is one of the strongest dramas since "East Lynne." Thrilling situations abound and the comedy element is equally strong. The drama is strong in character parts, the plot including a blind man, an Englishman, who is not slow in every sense of the word, an Irishman, a Scotchwoman, a Creole maid and a charming soubrette, all of whom are star parts. The professional stage will find this a drawing and paying play—but amateurs can easily produce it. Price, 25 cents.

Hector.
Farce in One Act,
BY
MAURICE HAGEMAN.
Author of "First Kiss," "A Crazy Idea," Etc.

Six male, two female characters. Plays forty-five minutes. Costumes, one messenger boy's, man and woman servants, a dudish young man, a flashy Hebrew, and lady and gentleman's street dress. Scene, a well furnished reception room. This farce has been a great success among professionals. The situations are so funny they can not be spoiled by the most inexperienced actors. The dialogue keeps up a constant hurrah in the audience. Hector, the dog, forms the central idea of the plot of the play, but need not be seen at any time unless a suitable animal is at hand. Price, 15 cents.

NEW PLAYS, 1897-98.

Diamonds and Hearts,

Comedy Drama in Three Acts,

BY

EFFIE W. MERRIMAN.

Author of "Socials," "Pair of Artists," "Maud Muller," Etc., Etc.

Four male, five female characters. Plays two hours. Costumes of to-day for house and street. Three interior scenes. Each character in this play is original and life-like. The three pretty young ladies have each a marked individuality, as have also the young doctor and young villain. The bachelor farmer has no rival unless we except the leading roles in "Denman Thompson," and "Shore Acres." He is a homespun lovable man and the scene in his home with his equally attractive sister is one of the strongest in the play. The drama is full of comedy, pathos and country life of the most wholesome nature. The story possesses an intense dramatic interest. **Price, 25 cents.**

An American Harem,

Comedietta in One Act.

Two male, five female characters. Plays twenty minutes. Costumes are ordinary street dress, except travelling suit for one man and very elaborate house dress for the servant. Scene, a handsomely furnished parlor. Frank's young wife suddenly disappears from home in a fit of temper, at the same time that his old college chum as suddenly appears to pay him a visit. His Irish servant, his mother, his sister and his cousin, with the best intentions of helping him out of the scrape, present themselves as his wife and the fun that ensues is immense. The comic situations arising from these complications are unlimited and the way in which the bright and sparkling dialogue works them out, keeps the audience convulsed from first to last. It is a play which furnishes opportunity for the highest class of acting, but at the same time if the players simply walk through it, it will make a hit every time.

It is easily staged as no scenery is required and the costuming and properties are always at hand. Price, 15 cents.

NEW PLAYS, 1897-98.

A Modern Proposal,

Duologue In One Act,

BY

MARSDEN BROWN,

Author of, "A Bold Stratagem," "A Passing Cloud," Etc.

One male, one female characters. A drawing-room scene. Costumes should be ordinary evening dress. Plays fifteen minutes. The best performers will welcome this two part comedy with the greatest cordiality. It is entirely new and very novel in situation and dialogue. All the changes seemed to have been rung upon a "proposal" scene for a young man and woman but Mr. Brown surprises us with an entirely new one. The dialogue is the most refined comedy, under which is shown at times strong feeling. Price, 15 cents.

A Crazy Idea,

Comedy In Four Acts,

BY

MAURICE HAGEMAN,

Ten male, eight female characters. Costumes of to-day. One interior scene. Plays two and one-half hours. A jealous husband suddenly decides to put his house in the care of his nephew and take his wife and daughter to travel because he is possessed of the idea that his wife has a lover. The nephew is impecunious and a young colored friend persuades him to rent the house to roomers and take him for a servant. The fun then begins. Each lodger is a strong character part and they get themselves and their landlord and his servant into most amusing scrapes. However all ends well.

The one scene required makes it a play easily produced on any stage where there are sufficient exits. The dialogue is very strong and keeps every audience in roars of laughter from beginning to end. There is no better comedy written than "A Crazy Idea." Price, 25 cents.

NEW PLAYS, 1897-98.

All Due to the Management.

A Monologue for a Gentleman,

BY

HELEN M. LOCKE.

Author of " A Victim of Woman's Rights," Etc.

Plays fifteen minutes. Scene, a comfortable sitting-room with a writing table. Costume, first overcoat and hat, which when removed discloses a plain sack suit. A gentleman is left at home by his wife to keep house while she is in the country resting. He attempts to write a magazine article while attending to his household duties. The result is a wrecking of his self complacency, his work as an author and the tidiness of the house. He finally leaves to recuperate with his wife in the country. It is an A 1 monologue. Price, 15 cents.

A Pair of Lunatics,

A Dramatic Sketch in One Act,

BY

W. R. WALKES.

Author of "Villain and Victim," "Rain Clouds," Etc., Etc

One male, one female characters. Plays fifteen minutes. Scene, a back parlor. Ordinary evening dress. This is among the most successful two-part sketches used at present. It is full of action and bright dialogue. The two characters mistake one another for lunatics and the fun that ensues is immense. This edition is well printed. Price, 15 cents.

A Passing Cloud.

A Monologue for a Lady.

BY

MARSDEN BROWN,

Author " Bold Stratagem," "A Modern Proposal," Etc.

Plays fifteen minutes. Handsome dinner costume and any pretty room. A handsome young woman is dressed for a dinner at her mother's house, and is waiting for her husband to return from business to accompany her. He is detained far beyond the time at which she expects him to arrive and she passes through a succession of emotions in consequence. This monologue can be presented before the most critical audiences with entire success. Price, 15 cents.

NEW PLAYS, 1897-98.

Conrad,

OR,

The Hand of a Friend.

Drama in Three Acts,

BY

FRANK DUMONT.

Author of "Undertaker's Daughter," "Too Little Vagrants," Etc.

Ten male, two female and one child characters. Plays two and one-half hours. Two exterior, one interior of hut scenes. Costumes modern and wild-western. This western drama is full of startling situations and thrilling incidents. It has been a most successful professional drama and pleases everybody and can be produced on a large or small stage. The book of the play gives the most minute stage directions, which have all been tried for several seasons on the regular professional stage. Repertoire companies will find this play a "winner," while amateurs will find it entirely free from anything objectionable in dialogue and a play that is easily produced. Conrad is a German character part which in the hands of a competent man may be made a star part, for he is given opportunity for much strong acting. However, there are six other strong characters. The Irish Servant and leading woman are good, and the Jew and the escaped convict, the half starved comedian are all excellent. Price, 25 cents.

By Telephone.

Sketch in One Act,

BY

MAURICE HAGEMAN.

One male, one female characters. Plays twenty minutes. Scene, a handsome room. Costumes of to-day, the gentleman any suit except evening dress; the lady, any elegant costume. This strong little comedy sketch is full of action and new business, full directions for which are given in the book of the play. The dialogue is refined and brilliant and will please all audiences. A wealthy young society man is introduced to the notice of a young woman with an income also, as a poor photographer. A mutual interest is developed and the scene played is when the young woman comes to his improvised studio to sit for her picture for which arrangements have been "by telephone." The situation it will be seen is new and novel and the dialogue is the most refined comedy. There is no finer twenty minute sketch for two people. Price, 15 cents.

NEW PLAYS, 1897-98.

Our Starry Banner,

Original Patriotic Drama in Five Acts,

BY

J. A. FRASER, JR.,

Author of "A Noble Outcast," "Modern Ananias," "Merry Cobbler," Etc.

Fifteen male, four female characters. Plays an entire evening. Costumes military and of the time of 1864. Three exterior, one interior scenes. By judicious doubling this piece can be played by eleven male and four female characters. The plot of this play is a romantic and absorbing story of the civil war. It is full of patriotism and the spirit of 1864, but there is nothing cheap or tawdry in either sentiment or plot. The author says: "The parts are all excellent and the leads are all on an absolute equality, Madge, Paul, Blackleigh, Dooley, the Squire, Judy, Millie and Will leaving little choice. Military organizations and Grand Army Posts will find this play exactly what they want, and Womans Relief Corps will see in Madge the only stage heroine who does justice to the noble part played by our women during these four years of untold anguish."

The piece affords a wealth of spectacular effect, at little or no expense. A military company is required and a brass band or fife and drum corps will add much to the effectiveness of Acts I and II. Price, 25 cents.

Joe,

Comedy of Child Life in Two Acts,

BY

CHARLES BARNARD,

Author of " County Fair," Etc.

Three male, eight female characters. Plays forty-five minutes. One interior and one exterior scenes. Costumes of to-day. This charming comedy introduces two mothers and nine children, from six to fourteen years of age. Micky Flynn, the bad boy and Joe, "the girl who likes boys," are great fun and every audience loves little Pussie and Dolly. The play depicts healthy every-day child life with exquisite touches. It is adapted to performance on a regular stage of a theatre or on a platform with or without scenery. The author's idea has been to make a play of real child life with child art and at the child's point of view. It may be played by adults representing children, but is better by real children. Price, 25 cents.